NIGHT OF THE LIVING DUMMY III

Look for more Goosebumps books
by R.L. Stine:
(see back of book for a complete listing)

Goosebumps®

NIGHT OF THE LIVING DUMMY III

R.L. STINE

AN
APPLE
PAPERBACK

SCHOLASTIC INC.
New York Toronto London Auckland Sydney

A PARACHUTE PRESS BOOK

No part of this publication may be reproduced in whole or in part, or stored in a retrieval system, or transmitted in any form or by any means, electronic, mechanical, photocopying, recording, or otherwise, without written permission of the publisher. For information regarding permission, write to Scholastic Inc., 555 Broadway, New York, NY 10012.

ISBN 0-590-56877-9

12 11 10 9 8 7 6 5 4 3 2 1   6 7 8 9/9 0 1/0

Printed in the U.S.A.   40

First Scholastic printing, February 1996

The stairs up to my attic are narrow and steep. The fifth step is loose and wobbles when you stand on it. All the other stairs creak and groan.

My whole house creaks and groans. It's a big, old house. And it's kind of falling apart. Mom and Dad don't really have the money to repair it.

"Trina — hurry!" my brother, Dan, whispered. His words echoed in the steep attic stairwell. Dan is ten, and he is always in a hurry.

He's short and very skinny. I think he looks like a mouse. He has short brown hair, dark eyes, and a pointy little chin. And he's always scurrying around like a mouse searching for a place to hide.

Sometimes I call him Mouse. You know. Like a nickname. Dan hates it. So I only call him Mouse when I want to make him mad.

Dan and I don't look at all like brother and sister. I'm tall and I have curly red hair and green eyes. I'm a little chubby, but Mom says not to worry about it. I'll probably slim down by the time I'm thirteen, next August.

Anyway, no one would ever call me Mouse! For one thing, I'm a lot braver than Dan.

You have to be brave to go up to our attic. Not because of the creaking stairs. Or the way the wind whistles through the attic windows and makes the panes rattle. Not because of the dim light up there. Or the shadows. Or the low ceiling covered with cracks.

You have to be brave because of the eyes.

The dozens of eyes that stare at you through the darkness.

The eyes that never blink. The eyes that stare with such eerie, heavy silence.

Dan reached the attic ahead of me. I heard him take a few steps over the squeaking, wooden floorboards. Then I heard him stop.

I knew why he stopped. He was staring back at the eyes, at the grinning faces.

I crept up behind him, moving on tiptoe. I leaned my face close to his ear. And I shouted, "BOO!"

He didn't jump.

"Trina, you're about as funny as a wet sponge," he said. He shoved me away.

"I think wet sponges are funny," I replied. I admit it. I like to annoy him.

"Give me a break," Dan muttered.

I grabbed his arm. "Okay." I pretended to break it in two.

I know it's dumb. But that's the way my brother and I kid around all the time.

Dad says we didn't get our sense of humor from him. But I think we probably did.

Dad owns a little camera store now. But before that he was a ventriloquist. You know. He did a comedy act with a dummy.

Danny O'Dell and Wilbur.

That was the name of the act. Wilbur was the dummy, in case you didn't guess it.

Danny O'Dell is my dad. My brother is Dan, Jr. But he hates the word junior, so no one ever calls him that.

Except me. When I want to make him *really* mad!

"Someone left the attic light on," Dan said, pointing to the ceiling light. The only light in the whole attic.

Our attic is one big room. There are windows at both ends. But they are both caked with dust, so not much light gets through.

Dan and I made our way across the room. The dummies all stared at us, their eyes big and blank. Most of them had wide grins on their wooden faces. Some of their mouths hung open. Some of their heads tilted down so we couldn't see their faces.

Wilbur — Dad's first dummy, the original Wilbur — was perched on an old armchair. His hands were draped over the chair arms. His head tilted against the chair back.

Dan laughed. "Wilbur looks just like Dad taking a nap!"

I laughed, too. With his short brown hair, his black eyeglasses, and his goofy grin, Wilbur looked *a lot* like Dad!

The old dummy's black-and-yellow checked sports jacket was worn and frayed. But Wilbur's face was freshly painted. His black leather shoes were shiny.

One wooden hand had part of the thumb chipped out. But Wilbur looked great for such an old dummy.

Dad keeps all of the dummies in good shape. He calls the attic his Dummy Museum. Spread around the room are a dozen old ventriloquist's dummies that he has collected.

He spends all of his spare time fixing them up. Painting them. Giving them fresh wigs. Making new suits and pants for them. Working on their insides, making sure their eyes and mouths move correctly.

These days, Dad doesn't get to use his ventriloquist skills very often. Sometimes he'll take one of the dummies to a kid's birthday party and put on a show. Sometimes people in town will invite him to perform at a party to raise money for a school or library.

But most of the time the dummies just sit up here, staring at each other.

Some of them are propped against the attic wall. Some are sprawled out on the couch. Some of them sit in folding chairs, hands crossed in their laps. Wilbur is the only one lucky enough to have his own armchair.

When Dan and I were little, we were afraid to come up to the attic. I didn't like the way the dummies stared at me. I thought their grins were evil.

Dan liked to stick his hand into their backs and move their mouths. He made the dummies say frightening things.

"*I'm going to get you, Trina!*" he would make Rocky growl. Rocky is the mean-faced dummy that sneers instead of smiles. He's dressed like a tough guy in a red-and-white striped T-shirt and black jeans. He's really evil-looking. "*I'm coming to your room tonight, Trina. And I'm going to GET you!*"

"Stop it, Dan! Stop it!" I would scream. Then I would go running downstairs and tell Mom that Dan was scaring me.

I was only eight or nine.

I'm a lot older now. And braver. But I still feel a little creeped out when I come up here.

I know it's dumb. But sometimes I imagine the dummies sitting around up here, talking to each other, giggling and laughing.

Sometimes late at night when I'm lying in bed, the ceiling creaks over my head. Footsteps! I picture the dummies walking around in the attic, their heavy black shoes clonking over the floorboards.

I picture them wrestling around on the old couch. Or playing a wild game of catch, their wooden hands snapping as they catch the ball.

Dumb? Of course it's dumb.

But I can't help it.

They're supposed to be funny little guys. But they scare me.

I hate the way they stare at me without blinking. And I hate the red-lipped grins frozen on their faces.

Dan and I come up to the attic because Dan likes to play with them. And because I like to see how Dad fixes them up.

But I really don't like to come up to the attic alone.

Dan picked up Miss Lucy. That's the only girl dummy in the group. She has curly blond hair and bright blue eyes.

My brother stuck his hand into the dummy's back and perched her on his knee. "Hi, Trina," he made the dummy say in a high, shrill voice.

Dan started to make her say something else.

But he stopped suddenly. His mouth dropped open — like a dummy's — and he pointed across the room.

"Trina — l-look!" Dan stammered. "Over there!"

I turned quickly. And I saw Rocky, the mean-looking dummy, blink his eyes.

I gasped as the dummy leaned forward and sneered. *"Trina, I'm going to GET you!"* he growled.

2

I uttered a startled cry and jumped back.

I swung around, ready to run to the attic steps — and I saw Dan laughing.

"Hey — !" I cried out angrily. "What's going on here?"

I turned back to see Dad climb to his feet behind Rocky's chair. He carried Rocky in one arm. Dad's grin was as wide as a dummy's!

"Gotcha!" he cried in Rocky's voice.

I turned angrily on my brother. "Did you know Dad was back there? Did you know Dad was here the whole time?"

Dan nodded. "Of course."

"You two are both dummies!" I cried. I flung my red hair back with both hands and let out an exasperated sigh. "That was so stupid!"

"You fell for it," Dan shot back, grinning at Dad.

"Who's the dummy here?" Dad made Rocky say. "Hey — who's pulling *your* string? I'm not a dummy — knock on wood!"

Dan laughed, but I just shook my head.

Dad refused to give up. "Hey — come over here!" he made Rocky say. "Scratch my back. I think I've got termites!"

I gave in and laughed. I'd heard that joke a million times. But I knew Dad wouldn't stop trying until I laughed.

He's a really good ventriloquist. You can never see his lips move. But his jokes are totally lame.

I guess that's why he had to give up the act and open a camera store. I don't know for sure. It all happened before I was born.

Dad set Rocky back on his chair. The dummy sneered up at us. Such a bad-news dummy. Why couldn't he smile like the others?

Dad pushed his eyeglasses up on his nose. "Come over here," he said. "I want to show you something."

He put one hand on my shoulder and one hand on Dan's shoulder and led us to the other end of the big attic room. This is where Dad has his workshop — his worktable and all his tools and supplies for fixing up the dummies.

Dad reached under the worktable and pulled up a large brown-paper shopping bag. I could tell by the smile on his face what he had in the bag. But I didn't say anything to ruin his surprise.

Slowly, carefully, Dad reached into the shopping bag. His smile grew wider as he lifted out a dummy. "Hey, guys — check this out!" Dad exclaimed.

The dummy had been folded up inside the bag. Dad set it down flat on the worktable and carefully unfolded the arms and legs. He looked like a surgeon starting an operation.

"I found this one in a trash can," he told us. "Do you believe someone just threw it away?"

He tilted the dummy up so we could see it. I followed Dan up to the worktable to get a better look.

"The head was split in two," Dad said, placing one hand at the back of the dummy's neck. "But it took two seconds to repair it. Just a little glue."

I leaned close to check out Dad's new treasure. It had wavy brown hair painted on top of its head. The face was kind of strange. Kind of intense.

The eyes were bright blue. They shimmered. Sort of like real eyes. The dummy had bright red painted lips, curved up into a smile.

An ugly smile, I thought. Kind of gross and nasty.

His lower lip had a chip on one side so that it didn't quite match the other lip.

The dummy wore a gray double-breasted suit over a white shirt collar. The collar was stapled to his neck.

He didn't have a shirt. Instead, his wooden chest had been painted white. Big black leather shoes — very scuffed up — dangled from his skinny gray pants legs.

"Can you believe someone just tossed him into the trash?" Dad repeated. "Isn't he great?"

"Yeah. Great," I murmured. I didn't like the new dummy at all. I didn't like his face, the way his blue eyes gleamed, the crooked smile.

Dan must have felt the same way. "He's kind of tough-looking," he said. He picked up one of the dummy's wooden hands. It had deep scratches all over it. The knuckles appeared cut and bruised. As if the dummy had been in a fight.

"Not as tough-looking as Rocky over there," Dad replied. "But he does have a strange smile." He picked at the small chip in the dummy's lip. "I can fill that in with some liquid wood filler. Then I'll give the whole face a fresh paint job."

"What's the dummy's name?" I asked.

Dad shrugged. "Beats me. Maybe we'll call him Smiley."

"Smiley?" I made a disgusted face.

Dad started to reply. But the phone rang downstairs. One ring. Two. Three.

"I guess your mom is still at that school meeting," Dad said. He ran to the stairs. "I'd better answer it. Don't touch Smiley till I get back." He vanished down the stairs.

I picked up the dummy's head carefully in both hands. "Dad did a great gluing job," I said.

"He should do *your* head next!" Dan shot back. Typical.

"I don't think Smiley is a good name for him," Dan said, slapping the dummy's hands together.

"How about Dan Junior?" I suggested. "Or Dan the Third?"

He ignored me. "How many dummies does Dad have now?" He turned back toward the others across the attic and quickly counted them.

I counted faster. "This new one makes thirteen," I said.

Dan's eyes went wide. "Whoa. That's an unlucky number."

"Well, if we count you, it's fourteen!" I said. Gotcha, Danny Boy!

Dan stuck out his tongue at me. He set the dummy's hands down on its chest. "Hey — what's that?" He reached into the pocket of the gray suit jacket and pulled out a folded-up slip of paper.

"Maybe that has the dummy's name on it," I said. I grabbed the paper out of Dan's hands and raised it to my face. I unfolded it and started to read.

"Well?" Dan tried to grab it back. But I swung out of his reach. "What's the name?"

"It doesn't say," I told him. "There are just these weird words. Foreign, I guess."

I moved my lips silently as I struggled to read them. Then I read the words out loud: "*Karru marri odonna loma molonu karrano.*"

Dan's mouth dropped open. "Huh? What's *that* supposed to mean?" he cried.

He grabbed the paper from my hand. "I think you read it upside down!"

"No way!" I protested.

I glanced down at the dummy.

The glassy blue eyes stared up at me.

Then the right eye slowly closed. The dummy *winked* at me.

And then his left hand shot straight up — and slapped me in the face.

3

"Hey — !" I shouted. I jerked back as pain shot through my jaw.

"What's your problem?" Dan demanded, glancing up from the slip of paper.

"Didn't you *see*?" I shrieked. "He — he *slapped* me!" I rubbed my cheek.

Dan rolled his eyes. "Yeah. For sure."

"No — really!" I cried. "First he winked at me. Then he slapped me."

"Tell me another one," Dan groaned. "You're such a jerk, Trina. Just because you fall for Dad's jokes doesn't mean I'm going to fall for yours."

"But I'm telling the truth!" I insisted.

I glanced up to see Dad poke his head up at the top of the stairs. "What's going on, guys?"

Dan folded up the slip of paper and tucked it back into the dummy's jacket pocket. "Nothing much," he told Dad.

"Dad — the new dummy!" I cried, still rubbing my aching jaw. "He *slapped* me!"

Dad laughed. "Sorry, Trina. You'll have to do better than that. You can't kid a kidder."

That's one of Dad's favorite expressions: "You can't kid a kidder."

"But, Dad — " I stopped. I could see he wasn't going to believe me. I wasn't even sure I believed it myself.

I glanced down at the dummy. He stared blankly up at the ceiling. Totally lifeless.

"I have news, guys," Dad said, sitting the new dummy up. "That was my brother — your uncle Cal — on the phone. He's coming for a short visit while Aunt Susan's away on business. And he's bringing your cousin Zane with him. It's Zane's spring vacation from school, too."

Dan and I both groaned. Dan stuck his finger in his mouth and pretended to puke.

Zane isn't our favorite cousin.

He's our *only* cousin.

He's twelve, but you'd think he was five or six. He's pretty nerdy. His nose runs a lot. And he's kind of a wimp.

Kind of a *major* wimp.

"Hey, stop groaning," Dad scolded. "Zane is your only cousin. He's family."

Dan and I groaned again. We couldn't help it.

"He isn't a bad kid," Dad continued, narrowing his eyes at us behind his glasses. That meant he was being serious. "You two have to promise me something."

15

"What kind of promise?" I asked.

"You have to promise me that you'll be nicer to Zane this time."

"We were nice to him last time," Dan insisted. "We *talked* to him, didn't we?"

"You scared him to death last time," Dad said, frowning. "You made him believe that this old house is haunted. And you scared him so badly, he ran outside and refused to come back in."

"Dad, it was all a joke," I protested.

"Yeah. It was a scream!" Dan agreed. He poked me in the side with his elbow. "A scream. Get it?"

"Not funny," Dad said unhappily. "Not funny at all. Listen, guys — Zane can't help it if he's a little timid. He'll outgrow it. You just have to be nice to him."

Dan snickered. "Zane is afraid of your dummies, Dad. Can you believe it?"

"Then don't drag him up here and scare the life out of him," Dad ordered.

"How about if we just play one or two little jokes on him?" Dan asked.

"No tricks," Dad replied firmly. "None."

Dan and I exchanged glances.

"Promise me," Dad insisted. "I mean it. Right now. Both of you. Promise me there will be no tricks. Promise me you won't try to scare your cousin."

"Okay. I promise," I said. I raised my right hand as if I were swearing an oath.

16

"I promise, too," Dan said softly.

I checked to see if his fingers were crossed. They weren't.

Dan and I had both made a solemn promise. We both promised not to terrify our cousin. And we meant it.

But it was a promise we couldn't keep.

Before the week was over, our cousin Zane would be terrified.

And so would we.

4

I was playing the piano when Zane arrived. The piano is tucked away in a small room in the back of the house. It's a small black upright piano, kind of beat-up and scratched. Dad bought it from my old music teacher who moved to Cleveland.

Two of the pedals don't work. And the piano really needs to be tuned. But I love to play it — especially when I'm stressed out or excited. It always helps to calm me down.

I'm pretty good at it. Even Dan agrees. Most of the time he pushes me off the piano bench so he can play "Chopsticks." But sometimes he stands beside me and listens. I've been practicing some nice Haydn pieces and some of the easy Chopin *études*.

Anyway, I was in the back of the house banging away on the piano when Zane and Uncle Cal arrived. I guess I was a little nervous about seeing Zane again.

Dan and I were really mean to him during his last visit. Like Dad said, Zane has always been scared of this old house. And we did everything we could to make him even *more* scared.

We walked around in the attic every night, howling softly like ghosts, making the floor creak. We crept into his bedroom closet in the middle of the night and made him think his clothes were dancing. We rigged a pair of Mom's panty hose so they cast a ghostly shadow of legs onto his bedroom floor.

Poor Zane. I think Dan and I went a little too far. After a few days, he jumped at every sound. And his eyes kept darting from side to side like a frightened lizard's.

I heard him tell Uncle Cal that he never wanted to come back here.

Dan and I laughed about that. But it wasn't very nice.

So I was a little nervous about seeing Zane again. I was playing the piano so loudly, I didn't hear the doorbell. Dan had to come running in and tell me Uncle Cal and Zane had arrived.

I jumped up from the piano bench. "How does Zane look?" I asked my brother.

"Big," Dan replied. "He grew. A lot. And he let his hair grow long."

Zane was always a pretty big guy. That's why Dan and I thought his being a total wimp was so funny.

19

He's big and beefy. Not tall. He's built kind of like a bulldog. A big blond bulldog.

I guess he's actually good-looking. He has round blue eyes, wavy blond hair, and a nice smile. He looks as if he works out or plays sports. He really doesn't look like the wimp type at all.

That's why it's such a riot to see him quivering in fear. Or wailing like a baby. Running to his mom or dad in terror.

I followed Dan through the back hall. "Did Zane say anything to you?" I asked.

"Just hi," Dan replied.

"A friendly 'hi' or an unfriendly 'hi'?" I demanded.

Dan didn't have time to answer. We had reached the front hall.

"Hey — !" Uncle Cal greeted me, stretching out his arms for a hug. Uncle Cal looks a lot like a chipmunk. He's very small. He has a round face, a twitchy little nose, and two teeth that poke out from his upper lip.

"You're getting so tall!" he exclaimed as I hugged him. "You've grown a lot, Trina!"

Why do grown-ups *always* have to comment on how tall kids are getting? Can't they think of anything else to say?

I saw Dad lugging their two heavy suitcases up the stairs.

"I didn't know if you'd be hungry or not," Mom

told Uncle Cal. "So I made a bunch of sandwiches."

I turned to say hi to Zane. And a flash of white light made me cry out in surprise.

"Don't move. One more," I heard Zane say.

I blinked rapidly, trying to clear the light from my eyes. When I finally focused, I saw that Zane had a camera up to his face.

He clicked it. Another bright flash of light.

"That's good," he said. "You looked really surprised. I only like to take candid shots."

"Zane is really into photography," Uncle Cal said, grinning proudly.

"I'm blind!" I cried, rubbing my eyes.

"I needed extra flash because this house is so dark," Zane said. He lowered his head to the camera and fiddled with his lens.

Dad came shuffling down the stairs. Zane turned and snapped his picture.

"Zane is really into photography," Uncle Cal repeated to my father. "I told him maybe you've got an old camera or two at the shop that he could have."

"Uh . . . maybe," Dad replied.

Uncle Cal makes a lot more money than Dad. But whenever he visits, he always tries to get Dad to give him stuff.

"Nice camera," Dad told Zane. "What kind of photos do you like to take?"

"Candid shots," Zane replied, pushing back his blond hair. "And I take a lot of still lifes." He stepped into the hall and flashed a close-up of the banister.

Dan leaned close and whispered in my ear, "He's still a pain. Let's give him a really good scare."

"No way!" I whispered back. "No scares this time. We promised Dad — remember?"

"I've set up a darkroom in the basement," Dad told Zane. "Sometimes I bring developing work home from the store. You can use the darkroom this week, if you want to."

"Great!" Zane replied.

"I told Zane maybe you have some sheets of developing paper you can spare," Uncle Cal said to Dad.

Zane raised his camera and flashed another picture. Then he turned to Dan. "Are you still into video games?" he asked.

"Yeah," Dan replied. "Mostly sports games. I have the new *NBA Jams*. And I'm saving my allowance to get the new thirty-two-bit system. You still play?"

Zane shook his head. "Not since I got my camera. I don't really have time for games anymore."

"How about some sandwiches, everyone?" Mom asked, moving toward the dining room.

"I think I'd like to unpack first," Uncle Cal told her. "Zane, you should unpack, too."

We all split up. Dan and Dad disappeared some-where. Uncle Cal and Zane went up to their rooms to unpack — our big old house has a lot of extra bedrooms.

I was heading into the kitchen to help Mom with the sandwiches when I heard Zane scream.

A shrill scream from upstairs.

A scream of horror.

5

Mom gasped and dropped the sandwich tray she was carrying.

I spun around and went running to the front hall.

Dad was already halfway up the stairs. "What's wrong?" he called. "Zane — what's the matter?"

When I reached the second floor, I saw Dan step out of his room. Zane stood in the hallway. Someone lay stretched across the floor at his feet.

Even from halfway down the hall, I could see that Zane was trembling.

I hurried over to him.

Who was sprawled on the floor like that, legs and arms all twisted?

"Zane — what happened? What happened?" Dad and Uncle Cal both shouted.

Zane stood there shaking all over. The camera seemed to tremble, too, swinging on its strap over his chest.

I glanced down at the body on the floor.

A ventriloquist's dummy.

Rocky.

Rocky sneered up at the ceiling. His red-and-white striped shirt had rolled up halfway, revealing his wooden body. One leg was bent under him. Both arms were stretched out over the floor.

"That d-dummy — " Zane stammered, pointing down at Rocky. "It — it *fell* on me when I opened the bedroom door."

"Huh? It *what*?" Uncle Cal cried.

"It dropped down on me," Zane repeated. "When I pushed the door. I didn't mean to scream. It just scared me, that's all. It was so heavy. And it fell near my head."

I turned and saw Dad glaring angrily at Dan.

Dan raised both hands in protest. "Hey — don't look at *me*!" he cried.

"Dan, you made a promise," Dad said sharply.

"I didn't do it!" Dan cried. "It had to be Trina!"

"Hey — no way!" I protested. "No way! I didn't do it!"

Dad narrowed his eyes at me. "I suppose the dummy climbed up on top of the door by himself!" he said, rolling his eyes.

"It was just a joke," Uncle Cal chimed in. "You're okay — right, Zane?"

"Yeah. Sure." Zane's cheeks were red. I could see he was embarrassed by all the fuss. "I just wasn't expecting something to fall on me. You know." He stared at the floor.

"Let's finish unpacking," Uncle Cal suggested. "I'm starting to get hungry." He turned to Dad. "Do you have any extra pillows? There's only one on my bed. And I like to sleep with a *lot* of pillows."

"I'll see if we have any more," Dad replied. He frowned at me. "You and Dan — take Rocky up to the attic. And no more little jokes. You promised — remember?"

I picked Rocky up carefully and slung him over my shoulder. "Get the attic door for me," I instructed Dan.

We made our way down the hall. "What is your problem, Mouse?" I whispered to my brother.

"Don't call me Mouse," he replied through gritted teeth. "You know I hate it."

"Well, I hate broken promises," I told him. "You can't wait one minute to start scaring Zane? You're going to get us in major trouble."

"Me?" Dan put on his innocent act. "I didn't hide the dummy up there. *You* did — and you know it!"

"Did not!" I whispered angrily.

"Hey, guys, can I come with you?" I turned to see Zane right behind us. I hadn't realized he'd followed us.

"You want to come up to the Dummy Museum?" I asked, unable to hide my surprise. Last visit, Zane had been afraid of the dummies.

"Yeah. I want to take some pictures," he replied. He raised his camera in both hands.

"Cool," Dan said. "That's a cool idea." I could see that he was trying to be friendly to Zane.

I didn't want to be left out. "It's neat that you're into photography," I told Zane.

"Yeah. I know," he replied.

Dan led the way up the attic stairs. Halfway up, I turned back. I saw Zane lingering at the bottom.

"Are you coming up or not?" I called down. My voice echoed in the narrow, dark stairwell.

I caught a look of fear on Zane's face. He was trying to be brave, I realized. Trying not to be afraid the way he was last time.

"Coming," he called up. I saw him take a deep breath. Then he came running up the stairs.

He stayed close to Dan and me as we crossed the attic. The eyes peered out at us darkly from around the big room.

I clicked on the light. The dummies all came into view. Propped on chairs and the old couch, leaning against the wall, they grinned at us.

I carried Rocky over to his folding chair. I slid him off my shoulder and set him down. I crossed his arms in his lap and straightened his striped shirt. The mean-looking dummy sneered up at me.

"Uncle Danny has a few new guys," Zane said from across the room. He stood close to Dan in front of the couch. He held the camera in his hands, but he didn't take any pictures. "Where does he find them?"

"He found the newest one in a trash can," I replied, pointing to the mean-looking dummy.

Dan picked up Miss Lucy and held it up to Zane. "Hiya, Zane! Take my picture!" Dan made Miss Lucy say in a high, shrill voice.

Zane obediently raised the camera to his eye. "Say cheese," he told Miss Lucy.

"Cheese," Dan said in Miss Lucy's high voice.

Zane flashed a picture.

"Give me a big wet kiss!" Dan made Miss Lucy say. He shoved the dummy's face close to Zane's.

Zane backed away. "Yuck."

"Put the dummy down," I told my brother. "We'd better get back downstairs. They're all probably waiting for us."

"Okay, okay," Dan grumbled. He turned to set Miss Lucy down. Zane wandered down the row of dummies, studying them.

I bent down and straightened Wilbur's bow tie. The old dummy was starting to look really ragged.

I was still working on the bow tie when I heard a hard *slap*.

And I heard Zane's startled cry of pain.

"Owwww!"

6

I spun around and saw Zane rubbing his jaw.

"Hey — that dummy *slapped* me!" he cried angrily.

He pointed to a red-haired dummy on the arm of the couch.

"I-I don't *believe* it!" Zane exclaimed. "It swung its arm up, and it — it *slapped* me!"

Dan stood behind the couch. I saw a smile spread over his face. Then he burst out laughing. "Get serious," he told Zane. "That's impossible."

"You did it!" Zane accused my brother, still rubbing his jaw. "You moved the dummy!"

"No way!" Dan backed away till he bumped the wall. "How could I? I was behind the couch the whole time."

I stepped quickly up to the couch. "Which dummy was it?" I demanded.

Zane pointed to a dummy with red hair and bright red freckles painted all over his grinning face. "That guy."

"Arnie," I reported. "One of Dad's first dummies."

"I don't care what his name is," Zane snapped. "He slapped me!"

"But that's dumb," I insisted. "It's just a ventriloquist's dummy, Zane. Here. Look."

I picked Arnie up. The old dummy was heavier than I remembered. I started to hand him to Zane. But my cousin backed away.

"Something weird is going on here," Zane said, keeping his eyes on the dummy. "I'm going to tell Uncle Danny."

"No. Don't tell Dad," I pleaded. "Give us a break, Zane. It'll get us in big trouble."

"Yeah. Don't tell," Dan chimed in. "The dummy probably just slipped or something. You know. It fell over."

"It reached up," Zane insisted. "I saw it swing its arm and — "

He was interrupted by Mom's voice from downstairs. "Hurry up, kids. Get down here. We're all waiting for you."

"Coming!" I shouted. I dropped Arnie back onto the arm of the couch. He fell into the dummy next to him. I left him like that and followed Dan and Zane to the stairs.

I held Dan back and let Zane go down by himself. "What are you trying to prove?" I angrily asked my brother. "That wasn't funny."

"Trina, I didn't do it. I swear!" Dan claimed, raising his right hand. "I swear!"

"So what are you saying?" I demanded. "That the dummy really reached up and slapped him?"

Dan twisted his face. He shrugged. "I don't know. I just know that I didn't do it. I didn't swing that dummy's arm."

"Don't be stupid," I replied. "Of course you did." I shoved my brother toward the stairs.

"Hey — give me a break," he muttered.

"You're a total liar," I told him. "You think you can scare Zane — and me. But it isn't worth it, Dan. We promised Dad, remember? Remember?"

He ignored me and started down the stairs.

I felt really angry. I knew that Dan had perched the dummy on top of the bedroom door so that it would fall on Zane. And I knew that he had swung the dummy's arm to slap Zane.

I wondered how far Dan would go to frighten our cousin.

I knew I had to stop him. If Dan kept this up, he'd get us both grounded for life. Or worse.

But what could I do?

I was still thinking about it in bed later that night. I couldn't get to sleep. I lay there, staring up at the ceiling, thinking about Dan and what a liar he was.

Dummies are made of wood and cloth, I told myself. They don't swing their arms and slap people.

And they don't get up and walk around the

house and climb up onto doors on their own. They don't walk on their own. . . .

They don't . . .

I finally started to drift off to sleep when I heard light footsteps on my bedroom carpet.

And then a hoarse whisper close to my ear: *"Trina . . . Trina . . ."*

7

"Trina . . . Trina . . . "

The hoarse whisper — so near my ear — made me shoot straight up in bed.

I leaped to my feet. Pulled the covers with me. Lurched forward.

And nearly knocked Zane onto his back.

"Zane?"

He stumbled backwards. "Sorry!" he whispered. "I thought you were awake."

"Zane!" I repeated. My heart thudded in my chest. "What are you *doing* in here?"

"Sorry," he whispered, backing up some more. He stopped a few inches in front of my dresser. "I didn't mean to scare you. I just — "

I held my hand over my heart. I could feel it start to slow back down to normal. "Sorry I jumped out at you like that," I told him. "I was half asleep, I guess. And when you whispered my name . . . "

I clicked on the bed-table lamp. I rubbed my eyes and squinted at Zane.

He was wearing baggy blue pajamas. One pajama leg had rolled up nearly to his knee. His blond hair had fallen over his face. He had such a frightened, little-boy expression on his face. He looked about six years old!

"I tried to wake up Dad," he whispered. "But he's such a sound sleeper. I kept knocking on his bedroom door and calling to him. But he didn't hear me. So I came in here."

"What's your problem?" I asked, stretching my arms over my head.

"I-I heard voices," he stammered, glancing to the open bedroom door.

"Excuse me? Voices?" I pushed my hair back. Straightened my long nightshirt. Studied him.

He nodded. "I heard voices. Upstairs. I mean, I *think* they were upstairs. Funny voices. Talking very fast."

I squinted at him. "You heard voices in the *attic*?"

He nodded again. "Yeah. I'm pretty sure."

"I'm pretty sure you were dreaming." I sighed. I shook my head.

"No. I was wide awake. Really." He picked up a little stuffed bear from my dresser. He squeezed it between his hands.

"I never sleep very well in new places," he told

me. "I *never* sleep very well in this house!" He let out an unhappy laugh. "I was wide awake."

"There's no one in the attic," I said, yawning. I tilted my ear to the ceiling. "Listen," I instructed. "Silent up there. No voices."

We both listened to the silence for a while.

Then Zane set down the stuffed bear. "Do you think I could have a bowl of cereal?" he asked.

"Huh?" I gaped at him.

"A bowl of cereal always helps calm me down," he said. An embarrassed smile crossed his face. "Just a habit from when I was a kid."

I squinted at my clock radio. It was a little after midnight. "You want a bowl of cereal *now*?"

He nodded. "Is that okay?" he asked shyly.

Poor guy, I thought. He's really freaked out.

"Sure," I said. "I'll come down to the kitchen with you. Show you where everything is."

I found my flip-flops and slipped my feet into them. I keep them under my bed. I don't like walking barefoot on the floorboards in the hall. There are a lot of nails that poke up from the floor.

Mom and Dad keep saying they're going to buy carpet. But money is tight. I don't think carpet is tops on their list.

Zane appeared a little calmer. I smiled at him and led the way into the hall.

He's not such a bad guy, I thought. He's a little wimpy — but so what? I decided to have a serious talk with Dan first thing in the morning. I planned to make Dan *promise* he wouldn't pull any more scares on Zane.

The long hall was so dark, Zane and I both held onto the wall as we made our way to the stairs. Mom and Dad used to keep a little night-light at the end of the hall. But the bulb burned out, and they never replaced it.

Holding onto the banister, we made our way slowly down the steps. Pale light from outside cast long blue shadows over the living room. In the dim light, our old furniture rose up like ghosts around the room.

"This house always creeps me out," Zane whispered, staying close by my side as we crossed through the front room.

"I've lived here all my life, and sometimes I'm scared of it, too," I confessed. "Old houses make so many strange sounds. Sometimes I think I hear the house groaning and moaning."

"I really did hear voices," Zane whispered.

We crept through the shadows to the kitchen. My flip-flops slapped on the linoleum. Silvery moonlight washed through the curtains over the kitchen window.

I started to fumble on the wall for the light switch.

But I stopped when I saw the dark figure slumped at the kitchen table.

Zane saw him, too. I heard Zane gasp. He jerked back into the doorway.

"Dad? Are you still up?" I called. "Why are you sitting in the dark?"

My hand found the light switch. I clicked on the kitchen light.

And Zane and I both let out a scream.

8

I recognized the red-and-white striped shirt. I didn't even have to see the face.

Rocky leaned over the table, his wooden head propped in his hands.

Zane and I crept closer to the table. I moved to the other side. The dummy sneered at me. His glassy eyes were cold and cruel.

Such a nasty expression.

"How did *he* get down here?" Zane asked. He stared hard at the dummy, as if expecting the dummy to answer.

"Only one way," I murmured. "He sure didn't walk."

Zane turned to me. "You mean Dan?"

I sighed. "Of course. Who else? Mister Dumb Jokes."

"But how did your brother know we'd be coming down to the kitchen tonight?" Zane asked.

"Let's go ask him," I replied.

I knew Dan was awake. Probably sitting on the

edge of his bed, waiting eagerly to hear us scream from the kitchen. Giggling to himself. So pleased with himself.

So pleased that he broke his promise to Dad. And gave Zane and me a little scare.

I balled both hands into tight fists. I could feel the anger rising in my chest.

When I get really furious like that, I usually go to the back room and pound the piano. I pound out a Sousa march or a hard, fast rock song. I pound the keys till I start to calm down.

Tonight, I decided, I would pound my brother instead.

"Come on," I urged Zane. "Upstairs."

I took one last glance at Rocky, slouched over the kitchen table. The dummy stared blankly back at me.

I really hate that dummy, I thought. I'm going to ask Dad to put him away in a closet or a trunk.

I forced myself to turn away from the sneering, wooden face. Then I put both hands on Zane's shoulders and guided him back to the stairs.

"I'm going to tell Dan that we're both fed up with his dumb jokes," I whispered to my cousin. "Enough is enough. We'll make him promise to stop leaving that dummy everywhere we go."

Zane didn't reply. In the dim light, I could see the grim expression on his face.

I wondered what he was thinking about. Was he remembering his last visit to our house? Was he remembering how Dan and I terrified him then?

Maybe he doesn't trust me, either, I told myself.

We climbed the stairs and crept down the dark hallway to my brother's room.

The door was half open. I pushed it open the rest of the way and stepped inside. Zane kept close behind me.

I expected Dan to be sitting up, waiting for us. I expected to see him grinning, enjoying his little joke.

Silvery moonlight flooded in through his double windows. From the doorway, I could see him clearly. Lying on his side in bed. Covers up to his chin. Eyes tightly closed.

Was he faking? Was he really awake?

"Dan," I whispered. "Da-an."

He didn't move. His eyes didn't open.

"Dan — I'm coming to *tickle* you!" I whispered. He could never keep a straight face when I threatened him. Dan is *very* ticklish.

But he didn't move.

Zane and I crept closer. Up to the bed. We both stood over my brother, staring hard at him, studying him in the silvery light.

He was breathing softly, in a steady rhythm. His mouth was open a little. He made short whistling sounds. Mouse sounds. With his pointy chin and upturned nose, he really did look like a little mouse.

I leaned over him. "Da-an, get ready to be tickled!" I whispered.

I leaned back, expecting him to leap out at me, to shout "Boo!" or something.

But he continued sleeping, whistling softly with each breath.

I turned to Zane, who hung back in the center of the room. "He's really asleep," I reported.

"Let's go back to our rooms," Zane replied in a soft whisper. He yawned.

I followed him to the bedroom door. "What about your cereal?" I asked.

"Forget it. I'm too sleepy now."

We were nearly to the door when I heard someone move in the hall.

"Ohhh." I let out a low moan as a face appeared in the doorway.

Rocky's face.

He had followed us upstairs!

9

I grabbed Zane's arm. We both shouted cries of surprise.

The dummy moved quickly into the room.

I cut my cry short as I saw that he wasn't walking on his own. He was being carried.

Dad had the dummy by the back of the neck.

"Hey — what's going on?" Dan called sleepily from behind us. He raised his head from the pillow and squinted at us. "Huh? What's everybody doing in my room?"

"That's what *I'd* like to know," Dad said sharply. He gazed suspiciously from Zane to me.

"You — you woke me up," Dan murmured. He cleared his throat. Then he propped himself up on one elbow. "Why are you carrying that dummy, Dad?"

"Perhaps one of you would like to answer that question," Dad growled. He had pulled a robe over his pajamas. His hair was matted to his forehead.

He wasn't wearing his glasses, so he squinted at us.

"What's going on? I don't understand," Dan said sleepily. He rubbed his eyes.

Was he putting on an act? I wondered. His innocent-little-boy act?

"I heard noises downstairs," Dad said, shifting Rocky to his other hand. "I went down to see what was going on. I found this dummy sitting at the kitchen table."

"I didn't put him there!" Dan cried, suddenly wide awake. "Really. I didn't!"

"Neither did Zane or me!" I chimed in.

Dad turned to me. He sighed. "I'm really sleepy. I don't like these jokes in the middle of the night."

"But I didn't do it!" I cried.

Dad squinted hard at me. He really couldn't see at all without his glasses. "Do I have to punish you and your brother?" he demanded. "Do I have to ground you? Or keep you from going away to camp this summer?"

"*No!*" Dan and I both cried at once. Dan and I were both going to summer camp for the first time this year. It's all we've talked about since Christmas.

"Dad, I was asleep. Really," Dan insisted.

"No more stories," Dad replied wearily. "The next time one of my dummies is somewhere he shouldn't be, you're both in major trouble."

"But, Dad — " I started.

"One last chance," Dad said. "I mean it. If I see Rocky out of the attic again, you've both *had* it!" He waved Zane and me to the door. "Get to your rooms. Now. Not another word."

"Do you believe me or not?" Dan demanded.

"I don't believe that Rocky has been moving around the house on his own," Dad replied. "Now lie down and get back to sleep, Dan. I'm giving you one last chance. Don't blow it."

Dad followed Zane and me into the hall. "See you in the morning," he murmured. He made his way to the attic stairs to take Rocky back up to the Dummy Museum. I heard him muttering to himself all the way up the stairs.

I said good night to Zane and headed to my room. I felt sleepy and upset and worried and confused — all at once.

I knew that Dan *had* to be the one who kept springing Rocky on Zane. But why was he doing it? And would he quit now — before Dad grounded us or totally ruined our summer?

I fell asleep, still asking myself question after question.

The next morning, I woke up early. I pulled on jeans and a sweatshirt and hurried downstairs for breakfast.

And there sat Rocky at the kitchen table.

10

I peered around the kitchen. No one else around.

How lucky that I was the first one downstairs!

I grabbed Rocky up by the back of the neck. Then I tucked him under one arm and dragged him up to the attic as fast as I could.

When I returned to the kitchen a few moments later, Mom had already started breakfast.

Whew! A close call.

"Trina — you're up early," Mom said, filling the coffee maker with water. "Are you okay?"

I glanced at the table. I had the sick feeling that Rocky would be sitting there sneering at me.

But of course he was upstairs in the attic. I had just carried him up there.

The table stood empty.

"I'm fine," I told her. "Just fine."

It was definitely Be Kind to Zane Day.

After breakfast, Dad hurried off to the camera

store. A short while later, Mom and Uncle Cal left for the mall to do some shopping.

It was a bright morning. Yellow sunlight streamed in through the windows. The sky stretched clear and cloudless.

Zane brought down his camera. He decided it was a perfect day to take some photographs.

Dan and I expected him to go outside. But our cousin wanted to stay indoors and shoot.

"I'm very interested in moldings," he told us.

We followed him around the house. Dan and I had made a solemn vow to be nice to Zane and not to scare him.

After breakfast, when Zane was upstairs getting his camera, I grabbed my brother. I pinned him against the wall. "No tricks," I told him.

Dan tried to wriggle away. But I'm stronger than he is. I kept him pinned against the wall. "Raise your right hand and swear," I instructed him.

"Okay, okay." He gave in easily. He raised his right hand, and he repeated the vow I recited. "No tricks against Zane. No making fun of Zane. No dummies — *anywhere*!"

I let him go as Zane returned with his camera. "You have some awesome moldings," Zane said, gazing up at the living room ceiling.

"Really?" I replied, trying to sound interested.

What could be interesting about a molding?

Zane tilted up his camera. He focused for what

seemed like hours. Then he clicked a photo of the molding above the living room curtains.

"Do you have a ladder?" he asked Dan. "I'd really like to get a closer shot. I'm afraid my zoom lens will distort it."

And so Dan hurried off to the basement to get Zane a ladder.

I was proud of my brother. He didn't complain about having to go get the ladder. And he'd lasted a whole ten minutes without cracking any molding jokes or making fun of Zane.

Which wasn't easy.

I mean, what kind of a nerd thinks it's cool to take photos of ceilings and walls?

Meanwhile, we had no school, and it was the sunniest, warmest, most beautiful day of March outside. Almost like spring. And Dan and I were stuck holding the ladder for Zane so he could use his macro lens and get a really tight molding shot.

"Awesome!" Zane declared, snapping a few more. "Awesome!"

He climbed down the ladder. He adjusted the lens. Fiddled with some other dials on the camera.

"Want to go outside or something?" I suggested.

He didn't seem to hear me. "I'd like to get a few more banister shots," he announced. "See the way the sunlight is pouring through the wooden bars? It makes a really interesting pattern on the wall."

I started to say something rude. But Dan caught my eye. He shook a finger at me. A warning.

I bit my lip and didn't say anything.

This is sooooo boring, I thought. But at least we're keeping out of trouble.

We stood beside Zane as he photographed the banister from all angles. After about the tenth shot, his camera began to hum and whir.

"End of the roll," he announced. His eyes lit up. "Know what would be really cool? To go down into the basement to the darkroom and develop these right now."

"Cool," I replied. I tried to sound sincere. Dan and I were both trying so hard to be nice to this kid!

"Uncle Danny said I could use his darkroom downstairs," Zane said, watching the camera as it rewound the film roll. "That would be awesome."

"Awesome," I repeated.

Dan and I exchanged glances. The most beautiful day of the *century* — and we were heading down to a dark closet in the basement.

"I've never watched pictures get developed," Dan told our cousin. "Can you show me how to do it?"

"It's pretty easy," Zane replied, following us down the basement stairs. "Once you get the timing down."

We made our way through the laundry room, past the furnace, to the darkroom against the far wall. We slipped inside, and I clicked on the special red light.

"Close the door tightly," Zane instructed. "We can't let in any light at all."

I double-checked the darkroom door. Then Zane set to work. He arranged the developing pans. He poured bottles of chemicals into the pans. He unspooled the film roll and began to develop.

I'd watched Dad do it a hundred times before. It really was kind of interesting. And it was cool when the image began to appear and then darken on the developing paper.

Dan and I stood close to Zane, watching him work.

"I think I got some very good angles on the living room moldings," Zane said. He dipped the large sheet of paper in one pan. Then he pulled it up, let it drip for a few seconds, and lowered it into the pan beside it.

A grin spread over his face. "Let's take a look."

He leaned over the table. Raised the sheet of paper. Held it up to the red light.

His grin faded quickly. "Hey — who shot this?" he demanded angrily.

Dan and I moved closer to see the photo.

"Who shot this?" Zane repeated. He furiously picked up another sheet from the developing pan. Another one. Another one.

"How did these get on the roll?" he cried. He shoved them all toward Dan and me.

Photos of Rocky.

Close-up portraits.

Photo after photo of the sneering dummy.

"Who shot them? Who?" Zane demanded angrily, shoving the wet photos in our faces.

"I didn't!" Dan declared, pulling back.

"I didn't either!" I protested.

But then, who did? I asked myself, staring hard at the ugly, sneering face on each sheet.

Who did?

11

"What's going on up here, guys?"

The dummies stared back at me blankly. None of them replied.

"What's the story?" I demanded. My eyes moved from one dummy to the next. "Come on, guys. Speak up or I'll come back here with a buzz saw and give you all haircuts!"

Silence.

I paced back and forth in front of them, gazing at them sternly, my arms crossed in front of my chest.

It was late in the afternoon. The sun had begun to lower itself behind the trees. Orange light washed in through the dusty attic windows.

I had crept up to the attic to search for clues. Something weird was going on.

How did all those photos of Rocky get onto Zane's roll of film? Who took those photos?

The same person who kept carrying Rocky

downstairs and sitting him where he would frighten Zane.

"It was Dan — right, guys?" I asked the wide-eyed dummies. "Dan came up here — right?"

I searched the floor. The couch. Under all the chairs.

I didn't find a single clue.

Now I was questioning the dummies. But of course they weren't being very helpful.

Stop wasting time and get back downstairs, I told myself.

I turned and started to the stairs — when I heard soft laughter.

"Huh?" I uttered a startled cry and spun around.

Another quiet laugh. A snicker.

And then a hoarse voice: *"Is your hair red? Or are you starting to rust?"*

"Excuse me?" I cried, raising a hand to my mouth. My eyes swept quickly from dummy to dummy.

Who said that?

"Hey, Trina — you're pretty. Pretty ugly!" That was followed by another soft snicker. Evil laughter.

"I like your perfume. What is it — flea and tick spray?"

My eyes stopped on the new dummy, the one Dad called Smiley. He sat straight up in the center of the couch. The voice seemed to be coming from him.

"Pinch me. I'm having a nightmare. Or is that really your face?"

I froze. A cold shiver ran down my back.

The hoarse voice *did* come from the new dummy!

He stared blankly at me. His mouth hung open in a stiff, unpleasant grin.

But the voice came from Smiley. The rude insults came from Smiley.

But that's impossible! I told myself.

Impossible!

Ventriloquist's dummies can't talk without a ventriloquist.

"Th-this is crazy!" I stammered out loud.

And then the dummy started to move.

12

I let out a scream.

Dan popped up from behind the couch.

The dummy toppled onto its side.

"You-you-you — !" I sputtered, pointing furiously at my brother.

My heart was pounding. I felt cold all over. "That's not funny! You — you scared me to death!" I shrieked.

To my surprise, Dan didn't laugh. His eyes were narrowed. His mouth hung open. "Who was making those jokes?" he demanded. His eyes darted from dummy to dummy.

"Give me a break!" I shot back. "Are you going to tell me it wasn't you?"

He scratched his short brown hair. "I didn't say a word."

"Dan, you're the biggest liar!" I cried. "How long have you been up here? What are you doing here? You were spying on me — right?"

He shook his head and stepped out from behind

the couch. "What are *you* doing up here, Trina?" he asked. "Did you come up to get Rocky? To take Rocky downstairs again and try to scare Zane?"

I let out an angry growl and shoved Dan with all my might.

He stumbled backwards and fell onto the couch. He cried out as he landed on top of the new dummy. He and the dummy appeared to wrestle for a moment as Dan struggled to climb to his feet.

I stepped up close to the couch and blocked his way. As he tried to get up, I pushed him back down.

"You know I'm not the one who's been moving Rocky around," I shouted. "We all know *you've* been doing it, Dan. And you're going to get the two of us in real trouble with Dad."

"You're wrong!" Dan declared angrily. His little mouse face turned bright red. "Wrong! Wrong! Wrong!"

He burst up from the couch. The dummy bounced on the cushion. Its head turned. It appeared to grin up at me.

I turned to my brother. "If you weren't planning more trouble, what were you doing up here?"

"Waiting," he replied.

"Excuse me? Waiting for whom?" I demanded, crossing my arms over my chest.

"Just waiting," he insisted. "Don't you *get* it, Trina?"

I kicked at a ball of dust on the floor. It stuck to the toe of my sneaker. "Get it? Get what?"

"Don't you see what's going on?" Dan demanded. "Haven't you caught on yet?"

I bent down and pulled the dust ball off my sneaker. Now it stuck to my fingers. "What is in your little mouse brain?" I asked. I rolled my eyes. "This should be good."

My brother stepped up beside me. He lowered his voice to a whisper. "Zane is doing it all," he said.

I laughed. I wasn't sure I'd heard him.

"No. Really." He grabbed my arm. "I know I'm right, Trina. Zane is doing everything. Zane is moving the dummy, bringing it downstairs, then pretending to be scared. Zane made it slap him. Zane carried it to the kitchen table both of those times."

I shoved Dan's hand off my arm. Then I spread my hand over his forehead and pretended to check his temperature. "You are totally losing it," I told him. "Go lie down. I'll tell Mom you're running a high fever."

"*Listen to me!*" Dan screeched. "I'm serious! I'm right. I know I'm right!"

"Why?" I demanded. "Why would Zane do that, Dan? Why would he scare himself?"

"To pay us back for last time," Dan replied. "Don't you get it? Zane is trying to get us in trouble."

I dropped down onto the couch beside Smiley. I thought hard about what my brother was saying. "You mean Zane wants Dad to think that you and I are using the dummies to scare Zane."

"Yes!" Dan cried. "But Zane is doing it all. He's scaring himself. And making it look as if we're doing it — to get us in big trouble."

I fiddled with the dummy's hand as I thought about it some more. "Zane scare himself? I don't think so," I replied finally. "What gave you this idea? What proof do you have?"

Dan dropped down on the couch arm. "First of all," he started, "you didn't carry Rocky downstairs all those times, did you?"

I shook my head. "No way."

"Well, neither did I," Dan declared. "So who does that leave? Rocky isn't walking around by himself — right?"

"Of course not. But — "

"It was the camera that gave it away," Dan said. "The photos Zane developed of Rocky were the biggest clue."

I let the dummy hand fall to the couch. "What do you mean?" I asked. I really wasn't following my brother's thinking at all.

"That camera is never out of Zane's sight," Dan replied. "Most of the time, he keeps it around his neck. So who else could have snapped all those photos of Rocky?"

I swallowed hard. "You mean that Zane — ?"

Dan nodded. "Zane was the only one who could have taken those pictures of Rocky. He sneaked up to the attic. He snapped them. Then he acted scared and angry when he developed them."

"But it was all an act?" I asked.

"For sure," Dan replied. "It's all been an act. To scare us. And to get us in trouble with Dad. Zane is trying to pay us back for how we scared him last time."

I still had my doubts. "It isn't like Zane," I argued. "He's so wimpy, so quiet and shy. He's not the kind of boy who plays tricks on people."

"He's had months to plan it!" Dan exclaimed. "Months to plan his revenge. We can prove it, Trina. We can hide up here and wait for him. That's why I was up here. Hiding behind the couch."

"To catch him in the act?"

Dan nodded. He whispered even though we were alone. "After everyone goes to bed tonight, let's sneak up here and wait. Wait and see if Zane comes."

"Okay," I agreed. "It's worth a try . . . I guess."

Was Dan right?

Would we catch Zane in the act?

I couldn't wait for everyone to go to sleep. I was dying to find out.

13

Gusts of wind rattled the attic windowpanes. Heavy clouds covered the moon.

We crept up the attic stairs into the darkness. Up a step. Then stop. Up a step. Then stop. Trying to be silent.

The old house moaned and groaned beneath us.

The attic stretched blacker than the stairway.

I reached for the light switch. But Dan slapped my hand away. "Are you crazy?" he whispered. "It has to be dark. Totally dark. Or else Zane will know that someone is up here."

"I know that," I whispered sleepily. "I just wanted to take one look at the dummies. You know. Make sure they're all here."

"They're all here," Dan replied impatiently. "Just keep moving. We'll hide behind the couch."

We crept on tiptoe over the attic floorboards. I couldn't see a thing. The heavy clouds kept any light from washing in through the windows.

Finally, my eyes adjusted to the darkness. I

could see the arms of the couch. I saw dummy heads. Dummy shoulders. Shadows against shadows.

"Dan — where are you?" I whispered.

"Back here. Hurry." His whisper came from behind the couch.

I could feel the dummy eyes on me as I made my way around the couch. I thought I heard a soft snicker. The evil laughter again.

But that had to be my imagination.

I trailed my hand over the couch arm. Felt a wooden dummy hand resting on the arm. The dummy hand felt surprisingly warm.

Humanly warm.

Don't start imagining things, Trina, I scolded myself.

That dummy hand is warm because it's *hot* up in this attic.

The wind rattled the glass. Strong gusts roared against the roof, so low over our heads.

I heard a loud groan. A soft chuckle. A strange whistling sound.

Ignoring all the attic noises, I ducked down on the floor beside my brother. "Well? Here we are," I whispered. "Now what?"

"Sssshhhh." In the darkness, I could see him raise a finger to his lips. "Now we wait. And listen."

We both turned and rested our backs against

the back of the couch. I raised my knees and wrapped my arms around them.

"He isn't coming," I whispered. "This is a waste of time."

"Ssshhh. Just wait, Trina," Dan scolded. "Give him time."

I yawned. I felt so sleepy. The heat of the attic was making me even sleepier.

I shut my eyes and thought about Zane.

At dinner, he couldn't wait to pass around the photographs of Rocky. "I don't know who took these shots," Zane complained to my dad. "But they wasted half a roll of film."

Dad glared angrily at Dan and me. But he didn't make a fuss. "Can we talk about it after dinner?" he suggested quietly.

"I'm kind of scared," Zane told Dad in a trembling voice. "So many weird things have been happening. It's like the dummies have lives of their own." He shook his head. "Wow. I hope I don't have nightmares tonight."

"Let's not talk about the dummies now," Mom chimed in. "Zane, tell us about your school. Who is your teacher this year? What are you studying?"

"Could I have a second helping of potatoes?" Uncle Cal interrupted. He reached for the bowl. "They're so good. I may have to make a pig of myself."

Dad took another quick glance at the close-up

snapshots of Rocky. He flashed Dan and me another angry scowl. Then he set the photos down on the floor.

After dinner, Dan and I were careful to keep as far away from Dad as we could. No way we wanted to hear another lecture about how we were terrifying our poor cousin. And how we'd be punished if we didn't stop it at once.

Now it was a little before midnight. And we were huddled in the dark attic. Listening to the swirling wind and the moans and groans of the house. Backs pressed against the couch. Waiting . . .

I kept my eyes closed. Thinking hard. Thinking about Zane. About Rocky.

Dan and I aren't alone up here, I thought drowsily. There are thirteen wooden dummies up here with us. Thirteen pairs of eyes staring into the heavy darkness. Thirteen frozen grins. Except for Rocky's sneer, of course.

Empty, lifeless bodies . . .

Heavy, wooden heads and hands . . .

Thinking about the dummies, the dummies all around, I guess I drifted off to sleep.

Did I dream about the dummies?

Maybe I did.

I don't know how long I slept.

I was awakened by footsteps. Soft, shuffling footsteps across the attic floor.

And I knew the dummies had come alive.

14

I jerked my head up, listening hard.

My hands were still wrapped around my knees. Both hands had fallen asleep. They tingled. The back of my neck ached. My mouth felt dry and sour.

I uttered a silent gasp as I heard the shuffling, scraping footsteps move closer.

Not dummies walking around, I realized.

A single figure. One. One person. Moving slowly, carefully toward the couch.

Why did I think I heard dummies moving? It must have been a picture left over from my dream.

I shook my hands, trying to make them stop tingling.

I was wide awake now. Totally alert.

The footsteps scraped closer.

Could it be Dan? Where was Dan?

Had he climbed up while I slept? Was he making his way back to the couch?

No.

Squinting into the darkness, I saw Dan beside me.

He had climbed to his knees. He saw me move. He waved his hand and signaled for me to be silent.

Dan gripped the back of the couch with both hands. Then he leaned forward and peered out into the room.

I crawled to the other end of the couch. Then, keeping low, I poked my head out and squinted into the deep shadows. All grays and blacks.

The wind howled around the house. Across the big attic room, the windowpanes rattled and shook.

I wanted to jump out. To scream and jump out. And flash on the light.

But I felt Dan's hand on my arm. He must have read my thoughts. He raised a finger to his lips.

We both waited. Frozen there behind the couch. Crouching low. Listening to each footstep. Each creak of the floorboards.

The dark figure stopped in front of the folding chair next to the couch. He stood inches from Dan and me. If I wanted to, I could reach out and grab his leg.

I struggled to see his face. But it was hidden by the couch. And I didn't dare raise myself up higher.

I heard the *clonk* of wood against wood. Two dummy hands hitting each other.

I heard the rustle of heavy cloth. The *thud* of leather shoes bumping each other.

The intruder had picked up a dummy off the chair.

Squinting into the deep blackness, I could see him swing the dummy over his shoulder. I could see the dummy arms swaying, swaying at his back.

The dark figure turned away quickly. And began walking to the attic stairs.

I crept out from behind the couch. Moving on tiptoe, I began to follow the intruder.

Pressed against the wall, tiptoeing as silently as I could, I moved across the room. I held my breath. I could hear Dan close behind me.

I reached the light switch just as the intruder made it to the stairs.

My hand fumbled against the wall as I reached.

Reached . . . reached for the light switch with a trembling hand.

Yes!

I flicked on the light. And Dan and I both shrieked at the same time.

15

"Zane!"

My brother and I both screamed his name.

Zane's eyes bulged. His mouth opened in a high, frightened wail.

I saw his knees bend. I think he nearly crumpled to the floor.

He uttered several squeaks. Then his mouth hung open. I could see he was gasping for breath.

"Zane — we caught you!" I managed to choke out.

He had Rocky draped over his shoulder.

"What — what — ?" Zane struggled to speak, but no words came out. He sputtered and started to choke. The sneering dummy bounced on his shoulder.

"Zane — we figured it out," Dan told him. "Your little tricks aren't going to work."

Our cousin was still sputtering and coughing.

"We know it's been you all along," Dan told him.

He stepped over and slapped Zane hard on the back a few times.

After a few seconds, Zane stopped sputtering.

Dan picked Rocky up off Zane's shoulder and started to carry him back to his chair.

"How-how-how did you know?" Zane stammered.

"We just figured it out," I told him. "What's the big idea, anyway?"

Zane shrugged. He lowered his eyes to the floor. "You know. Just having some fun."

I glared at him. "Some fun?" I cried angrily. "You tried to get us in huge trouble. You — you could have ruined our whole summer!"

Zane shrugged again. "It was kind of my turn. You know?"

"Well, we're even now," Dan chimed in.

"Right," I agreed quickly. "We're all even now — right, Zane?"

He nodded. "Yeah. I guess." A grin spread slowly over his face. "I had you guys going, didn't I? With that stupid dummy popping up everywhere you looked."

Dan and I didn't grin back.

"You fooled us," I murmured.

"You fooled everyone," my brother added.

Zane grinned. A gleeful grin. I could see how pleased he was with himself. "I guess Dan and I deserved it," I confessed.

"Guess you did," Zane shot back. Would he ever stop grinning?

"So now that we're even, do we have a truce?" I demanded. "No more joking around with the dummies? No more trying to scare each other or get anyone in trouble?"

Zane bit his lower lip. He thought about it a long, long time. "Okay. Truce," he said finally.

We all shook hands solemnly. Then we slapped each other high fives. Then the three of us started laughing. I'm not sure why. The laughter just burst out of us.

Crazy giggling.

I guess because it was so late and we were so sleepy. And we were so glad we could be friends now. We didn't have to play tricks on each other anymore.

As we made our way down the stairs, I felt really happy.

I thought all the scary stuff with the dummies was over.

I had no way of knowing that it was just beginning.

16

The next morning, Dan, Zane, and I went for a long bike ride. The strong winds had faded away during the night. A soft breeze, warm and fresh-smelling, followed us as we pedaled along the path.

The trees were still winter bare. The ground glistened with a silvery morning frost. But the sweet, warm air told me that spring was on its way.

We biked slowly, following a dirt path that curved into the woods. The sun, still low in the sky, warmed our faces. I stopped to unzip my jacket. And pointed to a patch of green daffodil leaves just beginning to poke up from the ground.

"Only three more months of school!" Dan cried. He raised both fists in the air and let out a cheer.

"We're going to camp this summer for the first time," I told Zane. "Up in Massachusetts."

"For eight weeks!" Dan added happily.

Zane brushed back his blond hair. He leaned

over the handlebars of my dad's bike and began pedaling harder. "I don't know what I'm doing this summer," he said. "Probably just hanging out."

"What do you *want* to do this summer?" I asked him.

He grinned at me. "Just hang out."

We all laughed. I was in a great mood and so were the guys.

Dan kept pulling wheelies, leaning way back and raising his front tire off the ground. Zane tried to do it — and crashed into a tree.

He went sailing to the ground, and the bike fell on top of him. I expected him to whine and complain. That's his usual style. But he picked himself up, muttering, "Smooth move, Zane."

"I want to see that one again!" Dan joked.

Zane laughed. "You try it!"

He brushed the dirt off his jeans and climbed back onto the bike. We pedaled on down the path, joking and laughing.

I think we were in such great moods because of the truce. We could finally relax and not worry about who was trying to terrify who.

The dirt path ended at a small, round pond. The pond gleamed in the sunlight, still half-frozen from the long winter.

Zane climbed off his bike and rested it on the tall grass. Then he stepped up to the edge of the pond to take photos.

"Look at the weeds poking up from the melting ice!" he exclaimed, clicking away. "Awesome. Awesome!" He knelt down low and snapped a bunch of weed photos.

Dan and I exchanged glances. I couldn't see what was so special about the weeds. But I guess that's why I'm not a photographer.

As Zane stood up, a tiny brown-and-black chipmunk scampered along the edge of the pond. Zane swung his camera and clicked off a couple of shots.

"Hey! I think I got him!" he declared happily.

"Great!" I cried. Everything seemed great this morning.

We hung out at the pond for a while. We took a short walk through the woods. Then we started to get hungry for lunch. So we rode back to the house.

We were about to return the bikes to the garage when Zane spotted the old well at the back of our yard. "Cool!" he cried, his blue eyes lighting up. "Let's check it out!"

Holding his camera in one hand, he hopped off his bike and went running across the grass to the well.

It's a round, stone well with green moss covering the smooth gray stones. It used to have a pointed red roof over it. But the roof blew off during a bad storm, and Dad hauled it away.

When we were little, Dan and I used to scare each other by pretending that monsters and trolls lived down inside it. But we hadn't paid much attention to the old well in years. Dad kept saying he was going to tear it down and cover it up. But he never got around to it.

Zane clicked a bunch of photos. "Is there still water down there?" he asked.

I shrugged. "I don't know."

Dan grabbed Zane around the waist. "We could toss you down and see if you make a splash!" he declared.

Zane wrestled himself out of my brother's grasp. "I've got a better idea." He picked up a stone and dropped it down the well.

After a long wait, we heard a splash far down below.

"Cool!" Zane exclaimed. He took several more pictures until he had finished the roll.

Then we made our way inside the house for lunch. We hurried upstairs to clean up.

Zane stopped at the doorway to his room.

I saw his eyes bulge and his mouth drop open. I saw his face go white.

Dan and I ran up next to him.

We stared into the bedroom — and cried out in horror.

17

"The r-room — it's been *trashed!*" Dan stammered.

The three of us huddled in the doorway, staring into the bedroom. Staring at an unbelievable mess.

At first I thought maybe Zane had left the windows open all night, and the strong winds had blown everything around.

But that didn't make any sense.

All of the clothes had been pulled out of the closet and tossed over the floor. The dresser drawers had all been pulled out and dumped over the carpet.

The bookshelves had been emptied. Books littered the floor, the bed — they were tossed everywhere. One bed table was turned on its side. The other stood upside down on top of the bed. A lamp lay on the floor in front of the closet. Its shade was ripped and broken.

"Look — !" Zane pointed into the center of the room.

Sitting on a tangled hill of clothes was Rocky. The dummy sat straight up, his legs crossed casually in front of him. He sneered at us as if daring us to enter.

"I-I really don't believe this!" I cried, tugging at the sides of my hair.

"*What* don't you believe?"

Mom's voice made me jump.

I turned to see her coming out of her bedroom. She tucked her blue sweater into her jeans as she walked toward us.

"Mom — !" I cried. "Something terrible has happened!"

Her smile faded. "What on earth — ?" she started.

I stepped aside so she could see into Zane's room.

"Oh, no!" Mom cried out and raised both hands to her cheeks. She swallowed hard. "Did someone break in?" Her voice sounded tiny and frightened.

I peered quickly into my room across the hall. "No. I don't think so," I reported. "This is the only room that's messed up."

"But — but — " Mom sputtered. Then her eyes stopped on Rocky on top of the pile of clothes. "What is *he* doing down here?" Mom demanded.

"We don't know," I told her.

"But who *did* this?" Mom cried, still pressing her hands against her cheeks.

"We didn't!" Dan declared.

"We've been outside all morning," Zane added breathlessly. "It wasn't Trina, or Dan, or me. We weren't home. We were riding bikes."

"But — someone had to do this!" Mom declared. "Someone deliberately tore this room apart."

But who was it? I wondered. My eyes darted around the mess, landing on the sneering dummy.

Who was it?

18

We all pitched in and helped get the room back together. It took the rest of the afternoon.

The lamp in front of the closet was broken. Everything else just had to be picked up and put back where it belonged.

We worked in silence. None of us knew what to say.

At first, Mom wanted to call the police. But there was no sign that someone had broken into the house. All the other rooms were perfectly okay.

Dad returned home from the camera shop while we were still cleaning up. He, of course, was furious. "What do I have to do? Bolt the attic door?" he shouted at Dan and me.

He grabbed up Rocky and slung the dummy over his shoulder. "This isn't a joke anymore," Dad said, narrowing his eyes at both of us. "This isn't funny. This is serious."

"But we didn't do it!" I protested for the hundredth time.

"Well, the dummy didn't do it," Dad shot back. "That's one thing I know for sure."

I don't know *anything* for sure, I thought. I stared at Rocky's sneering face as Dad started down the hall to the attic stairs. Then I bent down to pick up the broken lamp from the floor.

That night I dreamed once again about ventriloquist's dummies.

I saw them dancing. A dozen of them. All of Dad's dummies from upstairs.

I saw them dancing in Zane's room. Dancing over the tangled piles of clothes and books. Dancing over the bed. Over the toppled bed table.

I saw Rocky dancing with Miss Lucy. I saw Wilbur doing a frantic, crazy dance on top of the dresser. And I saw Smiley, the new dummy, clapping his wooden hands, bobbing his head, grinning, grinning from the middle of the room as the other dummies danced around him.

They waved their big hands over their heads. Their skinny legs twisted and bent.

They danced in silence. No music. No sound at all.

And as their bodies twisted and swayed, their faces remained frozen. They grinned at one another with blank, unblinking eyes. Grinned their frightening, red-lipped grins.

Bobbed and bent, tilted and swayed, grinning, grinning, grinning the whole time in the eerie silence.

And then the grins faded as I pulled myself out of the dream.

I opened my eyes. Slowly woke up.

Felt the heavy hands on my neck.

Stared up into Rocky's ugly face.

Rocky on top of me. The dummy on top of my blanket. Over me.

Reaching. Reaching his heavy wooden hands for my throat!

19

I opened my mouth in a shrill scream of horror.

My hands shot out. I grabbed the dummy's hands.

I thrashed my legs. Kicked off the blanket. Kicked at the dummy.

The big eyes stared at me as if startled.

I grabbed his head. Shoved him down.

I sat up, my entire body trembling. Then I grabbed the dummy's waist.

And flung him to the floor.

The ceiling light flashed on. Mom and Dad burst into my room together.

"What's happening?"

"Trina — what's wrong?"

They both stopped short when they saw the dummy sprawled on the floor beside my bed.

"He — he — " I gasped, pointing down at Rocky. I struggled to catch my breath. "Rocky — he jumped on me. He tried to choke me. I-I woke up and — "

Dad let out a loud growl and tore at his hair. "This has got to stop!" he bellowed.

Mom dropped down beside me on the bed and wrapped me in a hug. I couldn't stop my shoulders from trembling.

"It was so scary!" I choked out. "I woke up — and there he was!"

"This is out of control!" Dad screamed, shaking his fist in the air. "Out of control!"

Mom calmed me down. Then she and I both had to calm Dad down.

Finally, after everyone was calm, they turned out the light and made their way out of the room. They closed the door. I heard Dad carrying Rocky back up to the attic.

Maybe Dad *should* get a lock for the attic door, I thought.

I shut my eyes and tried not to think about Rocky, or Zane, or the dummies — or anything at all.

After a while, I must have drifted back to sleep. I don't know how much time passed.

I was awakened by a knock on the door. Two sharp knocks and then two more.

I sat straight up with a gasp.

I knew that Rocky had come back.

20

The bedroom door creaked open slowly.

I took a deep breath and held it, staring through the dark.

"Trina — ?" a voice whispered. "Trina — are you awake?"

As the door opened, a rectangle of gray light spilled into the room from the hallway. Dan poked his head in, then took a few steps across the floor.

"Trina? It's me."

I let out my breath in a long *whoosh*. "Dan — what do you want?" My voice was hoarse from sleep.

"I heard everything," Dan said, stepping up beside the bed. He pulled down one pajama sleeve. Then he raised his eyes to me. "Zane put Rocky on your bed. Zane did it!" Dan whispered.

"Huh? Why do you say that? We all have a truce — remember? Zane agreed the tricks were all over."

"Right," Dan whispered. "And now Zane thinks

he can *really* scare us. Because we don't suspect him any longer. Zane hasn't given up, Trina. I'm sure of it."

I bit my lower lip. I tried to think about what Dan was saying. But I was so sleepy!

Dan leaned close and whispered excitedly. "This morning before we went biking, Zane went up to his room — remember? He said he forgot his camera. So . . . he had time to mess up his room. Before he left the house."

"Yeah. Maybe," I murmured.

"And tonight he brought Rocky down and set him up on your bed. I'm sure of it," Dan insisted. "I'm sure it's Zane. We have to hide up in the attic again. Tomorrow night. We'll catch Zane again. I know we will."

"Hide up there again? No way!" I cried. "It's hot up there. And too creepy. And I'm staying as far away from those dummies as I can."

My brother sighed. "I know I'm right," he whispered.

"I don't know *what* I know," I replied. "I don't know anything about anything." I slid under the covers, pulled the blanket over my head, and tried to get back to sleep.

The next night, Mom and Dad had a dinner party in honor of Zane and Uncle Cal. They invited the Birches and the Canfields from down the street, and Cousin Robin and her husband Fred.

Fred is a great guy. Everyone calls him Froggy because he can puff out his cheeks like a frog. Froggy is short and very round and really looks like a frog.

He always makes me laugh. He knows a million great jokes. Robin is always trying to get him to shut up. But he never does.

Mom and Dad don't have many dinner parties. So they had to work all day to get the dining room ready. To set the table. And to cook the dinner.

Mom made a leg of lamb. Dad cooked up his specialty — Caribbean-style scalloped potatoes. Very spicy.

Mom bought flowers for the table. She and Dad brought out all the fancy plates and glasses that we usually see only on holidays.

The dining room really looked awesome as we all sat down to dinner. Dan, Zane, and I were down at the far end of the table. Froggy sat at our end. I guess, because he's just a big kid.

Froggy told me a moron joke. Someone asks a moron: "Can you stand on your head?" And the moron says, "No, I can't. It's up too high."

I started to laugh when I saw Zane jump up from the table. "Where are you going?" I called after him.

Zane turned back at the dining room doorway. "To get my camera," he replied. "I want to take some pictures of the table before it gets all messed up."

He disappeared upstairs.

A few seconds later, we all heard him scream.

Chairs scraped the floor as everyone jumped up. We all went running up the stairs.

I reached Zane's room first. From the doorway, I saw him standing in the center of the room.

I saw the sick look on Zane's face.

And then I saw the camera in his hand.

Or what was left of the camera.

It looked as if it had been run over by a truck. The film door had been twisted off and lay on the floor. The lens was smashed. The whole camera body was bent and broken.

Zane turned the camera over in his hands, gazing down at it sadly, shaking his head.

I raised my eyes to the bed. And saw Rocky sitting on the bedspread. A roll of gray film unspooled across his lap.

Dad burst into the room. All of our other guests pushed in after him.

"What happened?" someone asked.

"Is that Zane's camera?"

"What's going on?"

"That's what happens when you try to take my picture!" Froggy joked.

No one laughed. It wasn't funny.

Dad's face turned dark red as he took the camera from Zane's hand. Dad examined it carefully. His expression remained grim.

"This isn't mischief anymore," he murmured. I could barely hear him over all the other voices in the room. Everyone had begun talking at once.

"This cannot be allowed," Dad said solemnly. He raised his eyes to Dan, then me. He stared at us both for the longest time without saying anything.

Zane let out a long sigh. I turned and saw that he was about to cry.

"Zane — " I started.

But he uttered an angry shout. Then he pushed past Froggy and Mr. and Mrs. Birch. And went running from the room.

"Someone here has done a very sick thing," Dad said sadly. He raised the camera to his face, running a finger over the broken lens. "This is a very expensive camera. It was Zane's most prized possession."

All of our guests became very quiet.

Dad kept his eyes on Dan and me. He started to say something else.

But then we all heard the deafening crash from downstairs.

21

"What is going *on* here?" Dad cried. He tossed the broken camera onto the bed and darted from the room.

The others went hurrying after him. All talking at once. I heard their shoes pounding down the stairs.

I turned to Dan. "Still think Zane is doing these things?"

Dan shrugged. "Maybe."

"No way," I told him. "No way Zane is going to smash his own camera. He loved his camera. No way he would smash it just to get you and me in trouble."

Dan raised troubled eyes to me. "Then I don't get it," he said in a tiny voice. I could see the fear on his face.

I heard startled shouts and cries of alarm from downstairs. "Let's check out the *next* disaster," I said, rolling my eyes.

We reached the bedroom door at the same time

and squeezed through together. Then I led the way along the hall and down the stairs.

I fought back my own fear as we approached the dining room.

Something very strange was going on in this house, I knew. Dad was right when he said it was no joke.

Tearing Zane's room apart wasn't a joke. It was evil.

Wrecking Zane's camera was evil, too.

Thinking about Rocky gave me a chill. The dummy was always there. Whenever something evil happened, there sat Rocky.

Trina, don't be crazy! I scolded myself. Don't start thinking that a wooden ventriloquist's dummy can be evil.

That's crazy thinking. That's really messed up.

But what could I think?

My throat tightened. My mouth suddenly felt very dry.

I took a deep breath and led the way into the dining room.

I saw Dad in the kitchen doorway. He had his arm around Mom's shoulders. Mom had her head buried against Dad's shirtsleeve.

Was she crying?

Yes.

The guests all stood against the wall, shaking their heads, their expressions grim and confused. They muttered quietly, staring at the disaster.

The disaster. The terrible disaster.

The dining room table.

I saw the overturned platters first. Dad's scalloped potatoes smeared over the tablecloth. Clumps of potatoes stuck to the wall and the front of the china hutch.

The salad poured over the floor and the chairs. The bread ripped into small chunks, the chunks tossed over the table. The flowers ripped off their stems. The vase on its side, water pouring over the tablecloth, puddling on the floor.

The glasses all turned over. A bottle of red wine tipped over, a dark red stain spreading over the tablecloth.

I heard Mom's sobs. I heard the sounds of Dad's muttered attempts to calm her down. I saw the other guests shaking their heads, their faces so upset, so concerned, so puzzled.

And then Dan grabbed my shoulder and pointed me toward the head of the table. And I saw two dummies sitting there on dining room chairs.

Wilbur and the new dummy. Wilbur and Smiley.

They sat at the table, grinning at each other, wine glasses in their hands. As if celebrating. As if toasting each other.

22

That night, Dan and I hid behind the couch in the attic once again. The attic stretched dark and silent. So dark, I could barely see my brother sitting beside me.

We were both in pajamas. The air was hot and dry. But my hands and my bare feet felt cold and clammy.

We talked softly, our legs stretched out on the floor, resting against the back of the couch. As we talked, we waited — and listened. Listened to every sound.

It was nearly midnight, but I didn't feel sleepy. I felt alert. Ready for anything.

Ready to catch Zane in the act once again.

This time, I brought my little flash camera with me. When Zane crept up here to carry one of the dummies downstairs, I'd snap his photo. Then I'd have proof to show Mom and Dad.

Yes, I finally decided that Dan was right. Zane had to be the one who was destroying our house.

Destroying our house and trying to scare everyone into thinking the dummies had come to life.

"But why?" I whispered to Dan. "Did we scare Zane so badly the last time he was here? So badly that he'll do *anything* to pay us back?"

"He's sick," Dan muttered. "That's the only answer. He's totally messed up."

"So messed up that he wrecked his own camera," I murmured, shaking my head.

"So messed up that he ran downstairs and trashed the dining room," Dan added.

The dining room. That's what convinced me that Zane was guilty.

All of us were upstairs in Zane's room, examining his broken camera.

Zane was the only other person downstairs.

Zane was the only person in the house who could have trashed the dining room and wrecked the dinner.

Of course he acted horrified and shocked. Of course he acted as if he didn't have a clue about what had happened.

What a sad, sad night.

The dinner guests didn't know what to say to Mom and Dad. It was such a frightening mystery. No one had an answer.

The guests helped clean up the mess. The food was ruined. It couldn't be eaten. No one felt like eating, anyway.

Everyone left as soon as the dining room was cleaned and cleared.

As the last guest left, I turned to Dan. "Uh-oh," I whispered. "Family Conference Time. We're in for a major lecture now."

But I was wrong. Mom hurried up to her room. And Dad said he was too disgusted to talk to anyone.

Uncle Cal asked if Dad would like him to take the car and pick up some fried chicken or hamburgers or something.

Dad just scowled at him and stomped away. He carried Smiley and Wilbur up to the attic. I heard him slam the attic door. Then he disappeared into the bedroom to help comfort Mom.

Zane turned to his dad. "I-I can't believe my good camera is smashed," he whimpered.

Uncle Cal placed a hand on Zane's shoulder. "I'll bet your uncle Danny has a new camera at his shop that he'll want to give you."

"But I liked my *old* camera!" Zane wailed.

And that's when I decided he was guilty. He's a phony, I decided. He's carrying on like this — putting on a show for Dan and me.

But I wasn't going to fall for it. No way.

I made sure I had film in my little camera. Then I grabbed Dan and we crept up to the attic to wait. To wait in the darkness and catch Zane.

To end the disasters in our house once and for all.

We didn't have to wait long.

After about half an hour, I heard the tap of soft footsteps on the attic floor.

I sucked in my breath. My whole body tensed, and I nearly dropped the camera.

Beside me, Dan raised himself to his knees.

My heart pounding, I crept to the edge of the couch.

Tap tap. Shuffling footsteps on the bare floorboards.

I saw a dark figure bend down and lift a dummy off a chair.

"It's Zane," I whispered to Dan. "I knew it!"

In the heavy darkness, I could see him carrying the dummy to the stairs.

I stood up. My legs trembled. But I moved quickly.

I raised the camera. Stepped in front of the couch.

Pushed the shutter button.

The room flashed in an explosion of white light.

I clicked off another one.

Another bright white flash.

And in the flash, I saw Rocky dangling over Zane's shoulder.

No.

Not Zane!

Not Zane. Not Zane.

In the flash of light, I saw Rocky dangling over *another dummy's* shoulder!

Smiley! The new dummy.

The new dummy was shuffling toward the stairs, carrying Rocky away.

23

The dummy turned.

My hand fumbled for the light switch. I clicked on the light.

I stood frozen in front of the couch. Too startled to move.

"Smiley — stop!" I screamed.

The dummy's grin faded. The eyes narrowed at me. "I'm not Smiley," he croaked. He had a hoarse, raspy voice. "My name is Slappy."

He turned back to the stairs.

"Stop him!" I cried to my brother.

We both made a dive for the dummy.

Slappy spun around. He pulled Rocky off his shoulder — and heaved him at Dan.

I grabbed Slappy around the waist and tackled him to the floor.

He swung both hands hard. One of them slammed into my forehead.

"Unh." I let out a groan as the pain shot through me.

My hands slid off the dummy's slender waist. Slappy jumped nimbly to his feet, his grin wide and leering.

He was enjoying this!

He kicked me in the side with the toe of his big leather shoe.

My head still throbbing, I rolled out of the way. And turned back in time to see Dan grab the dummy from behind.

Dan drove his head into the dummy's back. They both dropped hard to the floor.

"Let go of me, slave!" Slappy demanded in his ugly, hoarse voice. "You are my slave now! Let go of me! I order you!"

I pulled myself to my knees as Dan and Slappy wrestled over the floor.

"He's so . . . *strong!*" Dan called out to me.

Slappy rolled on top of him. Started to pound him with his wooden fists.

I grabbed Slappy by the shoulders and tugged with all my strength. Slappy swung his arms, thrashing at my brother.

I pulled hard, trying to tug him off Dan's stomach.

"Let go! Let go!" the dummy shrieked. "Let go, slave!"

"Get off him!" I cried.

We were making such a racket, I didn't hear the attic door open downstairs. And I didn't hear the footsteps running up the stairs.

A face appeared. And then a large body.

"Dad!" I cried breathlessly. "Dad — look!"

"What on earth — !" Dad exclaimed.

"Dad — it's alive! The dummy is alive!" I shrieked.

"Huh?" Squinting through his glasses, Dad lowered his gaze to the dummy on the floor.

The dummy sprawled lifelessly on its back beside Dan. One arm was twisted beneath its back. Both legs were bent in two.

The mouth hung open in its painted grin. The eyes stared blankly at the ceiling.

"It *is* alive!" Dan insisted. "It really is!"

Dad stared down at the still, silent dummy.

"The dummy picked up Rocky!" Dan declared in a high, excited voice. "He said his name was Slappy. He picked up Rocky. He was carrying him downstairs."

Dad *tsk-tsk*ed and shook his head. "Give it up, Dan," he murmured angrily. "Just stop it right now." He raised his eyes to Dan, then to me. "I knew you two were the troublemakers."

"But, Dad — " I protested.

"I'm not an idiot," Dad snapped, scowling at me. "You can't expect me to believe a dumb story about a dummy coming to life and carrying another dummy around. Have you both lost your minds entirely?"

"It's true," Dan insisted.

We both gazed down at Slappy. He sure didn't

look alive. For a moment, I had the frightening feeling that I'd dreamed the whole scene.

But then I remembered something. "I have proof!" I cried. "Dad, I can prove to you that Dan and I aren't lying."

Dad rubbed the back of his neck. "I'm so tired," he moaned. "It's been such a long, horrible day. Please. Give me a break, Trina."

"But I took some pictures!" I told him. "I have pictures of Slappy carrying Rocky!"

"Trina, I'm warning you — " Dad started.

But I spun away, searching for my camera. Where was it? Where?

It took me a few seconds to spot it on the floor against the wall back by the couch. I hurried across the room to grab it.

And stopped halfway.

The back of the camera — it had sprung open. The film was exposed. The pictures were ruined.

The camera must have flown out of my hand when I tried to tackle Slappy, I realized. I picked it up and examined it sadly.

No pictures. No proof.

I turned back to find Dad scowling at me. "No more wasting my time, Trina. You two are grounded until further notice. I'm so disgusted with both of you. Your mother and I will think of other punishments after your cousin leaves."

Then Dad waved a hand at Slappy and Rocky. "Put them away. Right now. And stay out of the attic. Stay away from my dummies. That's all I have to say to you. Good night."

Dad turned away sharply and stomped down the stairs.

I glanced at Dan and shrugged. I didn't know what to say.

My heart was pounding. I was so angry. So upset. So *hurt*. My chest felt about to explode.

I bent down to pick up Slappy.

The dummy winked at me.

His ugly grin grew wider. And then he puckered his red lips and made disgusting, wet kissing sounds.

24

"Don't touch me, slave," Slappy growled.

I gasped and jumped back. I still couldn't believe this was happening. I wrapped my arms around myself to stop my body from trembling.

"You — you really are alive?" Dan asked softly.

"You bet your soft head I am!" the dummy roared.

"What do you want?" I cried. "Why are you doing this to us? Why are you getting us in all this trouble?"

The ugly grin spread over his face. "If you treat me nice, slaves, maybe I won't get you in any more trouble. Maybe you'll get lucky." He tapped his head and added, "Knock on wood."

"We're not your slaves!" I insisted.

He tossed back his head and let out a dry laugh. "Who's the dummy here?" he cried. "You or me?"

"You carried Rocky downstairs all those times?" Dan asked. I could see that my brother was having a hard time believing this, too.

"You don't think that bag of kindling can move on his own, do you?" Slappy sneered. "I had some fun with that ugly guy. I put him at the scene of the crimes to throw you off the track. To keep you slaves guessing."

"And you smashed Zane's camera and ruined the dinner party?" I demanded.

He narrowed his eyes to evil slits. "I'll do much worse if you slaves don't obey me."

I could feel the anger rising through my body. "You — you're going to ruin everything!" I screamed at him. "You're going to ruin our lives! You're going to keep us from going to camp this summer!"

Slappy snickered. "You won't be going to camp. You'll be staying home to take good care of *me*!"

And then I exploded.

"Nooooo!" I uttered a long wail of protest.

I grabbed his head in both hands. I started to tug.

I remembered his head had been split in two when Dad found him. I planned to pull his head apart — to split it in two again!

He kicked his legs frantically and thrashed his arms.

His heavy shoes kicked at my legs.

But I held on tight. Pulling. Pulling. Struggling to pull his head apart.

"Let me try! Let me try!" Dan called.

I let out a sigh and dropped the dummy to the

floor. "It's no use," I told Dan. "Dad did too good a job. It's glued tight."

Slappy scrambled to his feet. He shook his head. "Thanks for the head massage, slave! Now rub my back!" He laughed, an ugly dry laugh that sounded more like a cough.

Dan stared at the dummy in wide-eyed horror. "Trina — what are we going to do?" he cried, his voice just above a whisper.

"How about a game of Kick the Dummy Down the Stairs?" Slappy suggested, leering at us. "We'll take turns being the dummy. You can go first!"

"We — we have to do something!" Dan stammered. "He's a *monster!* He's evil! We have to get rid of him!"

But how? I wondered.

How?

And then I had an idea.

25

Slappy must have read my thoughts. He turned and started to run.

But I dove fast — and wrapped my hands around his skinny legs.

He let out a harsh, angry cry as I began twisting his legs around each other, struggling to tie them in a knot.

He swung an arm. The wooden hand caught me on the ear.

But I held on.

"Dan — grab his arms! Hurry!"

My brother moved quickly. Slappy tried to bat him away. But Dan ducked low. And when he came up, he grabbed Slappy's wrists and held on.

"Let me go, slaves!" the dummy rasped. "Let me go now. You'll be sorry! You'll pay!"

I saw the fear on Dan's face.

Slappy swung a hand free. He tried to swipe at Dan's throat.

But Dan reached out and grabbed onto the loose arm again.

I felt eyes on me. I glanced up to see the other dummies around the room. They appeared to watch us struggle. A silent, still audience.

I pulled a red kerchief off a dummy's neck. And I stuffed it into Slappy's mouth to keep him quiet.

"Downstairs! Hurry!" I instructed my brother.

The dummy twisted and squirmed, trying to break free.

But I had his legs tied around each other. And Dan kept a tight grip on his arms.

We began making our way to the attic stairs. "Where are we taking him?" Dan demanded.

"Outside," I replied. The dummy bucked and squirmed. I nearly dropped him.

"In our pajamas?" Dan asked.

I nodded and began backing down the stairs. Slappy struggled hard to get free. I nearly lost my balance and toppled over backwards.

"We're not going far," I groaned.

Somehow we made it all the way downstairs. I had to let go with one hand to open the front door. Slappy bucked his knees, trying to untangle his legs.

I pushed the door open. Grabbed the legs again.

Dan and I carried the squirming dummy outside.

103

A cold, clear night. A light, silvery frost over the grass. A half moon high over the trees.

"Ohhh." I let out a moan as my bare feet touched the frozen grass.

"It's c-cold!" Dan stammered. "I can't hold on much longer."

I saw him shiver. The front lawn suddenly darkened as clouds rolled over the moon. My legs trembled. The damp cold seeped through my thin pajamas.

"Where are we taking him?" Dan whispered.

"Around to the back."

Slappy kicked hard. But I held on tightly.

Something scampered past my bare feet. I heard scurrying footsteps over the frosty ground.

A rabbit? A raccoon?

I didn't stop to see. Gripping Slappy's ankles with both hands, I backed up. Backed along the side of the house.

"My feet are numb!" Dan complained.

"Almost there," I replied.

Slappy uttered hoarse cries beneath the kerchief that gagged his mouth. His round eyes rolled wildly. Again, he tried to kick free.

Dan and I hauled him to the back of the yard. By the time we got to the old well, my feet were frozen numb, too. And my whole body shook from the cold.

"What are we going to do?" Dan asked in a tiny voice.

The clouds rolled away. Shadows pulled back. The silvery moonlight lit up the old stone well.

"We're going to toss him down the well," I groaned.

Dan stared at me, surprised.

"He's evil," I explained. "We have no choice."

Dan nodded.

We lifted Slappy onto the smooth stones at the top of the well. He bucked and kicked. He tried to scream through his gag.

I saw Dan shiver again.

"It's a wooden dummy," I told him. "It isn't a person. It's an evil wooden dummy."

We both shoved hard at the same time.

The dummy slid off the stone wall and dropped into the well.

Dan and I both waited until we heard the splash from far below.

Then we ran side by side back to the house.

He's gone! I thought gratefully. Joyfully. The evil thing is gone for good.

I slept really well that night. And I didn't dream about dummies.

The next morning, Dan and I met in the hall. We both were smiling. We felt so good.

I was actually singing as I followed Dan down the stairs for breakfast.

Dad greeted us at the kitchen door with an

angry frown. "What is *he* doing down here?" Dad demanded.

He pointed into the kitchen.

Pointed at the breakfast table.

Pointed to Slappy, sitting at the breakfast table, grinning his ugly painted grin, his eyes wide and innocent.

26

Dan's mouth dropped open.

I let out a sharp cry.

"Don't act stunned. Just get him out of here," Dad said angrily. "And why is he all wet? Did you have him out in the rain?"

I glanced out the kitchen window. Lightning flashed through a dark gray sky. Sheets of rain pounded the glass. Thunder rumbled overhead.

"Not a very nice morning," Uncle Cal said, stepping up behind Dan and me.

"I've got coffee ready," Dad told him.

"I see your friend here beat us down to breakfast," Uncle Cal said, motioning to Slappy.

The dummy's grin seemed to grow wider.

"Get him out of here, Trina," Dad repeated sharply. "Anyone want pancakes this morning?" He moved to the cabinet and started searching for a frying pan.

"Make a few extra for me. I'm starving," Uncle

Cal said. "I'll go see if Zane is up." He turned and hurried out of the kitchen.

Dad leaned into the cabinet, banging pots and pans, searching for the one he always used for pancakes.

"Dad, I have to tell you something," I said softly. I couldn't hold it in any longer. I had to tell Dad the truth. I had to tell him the whole story.

"Dad, Slappy is evil," I told him. "He's alive, and he's evil. Dan and I threw him down the well last night. We had to get rid of him. But now — he's back. You have to help us, Dad. We have to get rid of him — now."

I took a deep breath and let it out. It felt so good to get the story off my chest.

Dad pulled his head from the cabinet and turned to me. "Did you say something, Trina? I was making such a racket, I couldn't hear you."

"Dad, I-I — " I stammered.

"Get that dummy *out* of here — now!" Dad shouted. He stuck his head back into the cabinet. "How can a whole frying pan disappear into thin air?"

I let out a disappointed sigh. A loud burst of thunder made me jump.

I motioned with my head for Dan to help me. We lifted Slappy off the chair. I held him around the waist, as far away from me as possible.

His gray suit was sopping wet. Water dripped off his black leather shoes.

We were halfway up the attic stairs when Slappy blinked and let out a soft chuckle. "Nice try, slaves," he rasped. "But give up. I'm never going away. Never!"

27

What a dreary morning.

Rain pounded the windows. Lightning crackled through the charcoal-gray sky. Thunder boomed so close it rocked the house.

I felt as if the storm were inside my head. As if the heavy, heavy storm clouds were weighing me down. As if the thunder erupted inside my brain, drowning out my thoughts.

Dan and I slumped on the couch in the den, watching the storm through the venetian blinds over the big window. We were trying to come up with an idea, a way to get rid of Slappy.

The room was chilly. Damp, cold air leaked through the old window. I rubbed the sleeves of my sweater, trying to warm myself.

We were alone in the house. Mom, Dad, Uncle Cal, and Zane had gone into town.

"I tried to tell Dad," I said. "You heard me, Dan. I tried to tell him about Slappy. But he didn't hear me."

110

"Dad wouldn't believe you anyway, Trina," Dan replied glumly. He sighed. "Who *would* believe it?"

"How can a wooden dummy come to life?" I asked, shaking my head. "How?"

And then I remembered.

And then I had an idea.

I jumped up from the couch. I tugged my brother by the arm. "Come on."

He pulled back. "Where?"

"To the attic. I think I know how to put Slappy to sleep — for good."

I stopped at the attic door and held Dan back. "Be very quiet," I instructed him. "Maybe Slappy is asleep. If he's asleep, my plan will go a whole lot better."

Thunder roared as I opened the door. I led the way up the stairs, moving slowly, carefully, one step at a time. I could hear the rain pounding down on the roof. And I could see the flicker of lightning on the low ceiling.

I stopped as I reached the top of the stairs and turned toward the dummy collection. A flash of lightning through the window cast the shadows of their heads on the wall. As the lightning flickered, the shadows all seemed to be moving.

Dan stepped up behind me. "Here we are. Now what?" he whispered.

I raised a finger to my lips and began to tiptoe

across the floor. Thunder boomed. It sounded so much louder up here under the roof!

When Dan and I dragged Slappy up here this morning, we had tossed him down on the floor. We were too freaked and frightened to spend the time propping him up on his chair. We just wanted to dump him and get away from the attic.

I saw Slappy in the flickering white lightning. Lying on his back in the center of the floor. The other dummies sat around him, grinning their silent grins.

I took a step closer. And then another. Moving as silently as I could.

I peered down at the evil dummy. His arms were at his sides. His legs were twisted around each other.

And his eyes were closed.

Yes!

His eyes were closed. He was asleep.

I took another few steps toward Slappy. But I felt Dan's hand on my arm, tugging me back. "Trina — what are you going to do?" he whispered.

My eyes darted to Slappy. Still asleep. Thunder roared all around. It sounded as if we were standing in the middle of it.

"Remember those weird words I read?" I whispered to my brother, keeping my eyes on the evil dummy. "Remember those weird words on that slip of paper?"

Dan thought for a moment. Then he nodded.

"Well, maybe it was those words that brought him to life," I whispered. "Maybe it's some kind of secret chant."

Dan shrugged. "Maybe." He didn't sound too hopeful.

"I saw you tuck that slip of paper back into Slappy's jacket pocket," I told my brother. "I'm going to take it out and read the words again. Maybe the same words that bring him to life will also put him back to sleep."

Of *course* it was a crazy idea.

But a dummy coming to life was crazy, too. And a dummy trying to turn you into his slave was crazy.

It was *all* crazy. So maybe my idea was just crazy enough to work.

"Good luck," my brother whispered, his eyes on the sleeping dummy on the floor.

I made my way over to Slappy.

I knelt down on my knees beside him.

I took a deep breath and held it. Then slowly, slowly, I began to reach my hand down to his jacket pocket.

I knew the slip of paper was inside that pocket. Could I pull it out without waking up Slappy?

I lowered my hand. Lowered it.

My fingers touched the top of the jacket pocket.

Still holding my breath, I began to slip two fingers inside.

"Gotcha!" Slappy shrieked as his hands shot up. He grabbed both of my wrists and began to squeeze.

28

I was so stunned, I nearly fell on top of him.

As I struggled to keep my balance, his wooden hands dug into my wrists. They tightened around me, cutting into my skin.

"Let go of me!" I screamed. I struggled to pull my arms away. But he was too strong. Too strong.

The hard fingers dug into my wrists. They squeezed harder, harder — until they cut off all circulation.

"Let go of me! Let go!" My cry came out a shrill wail.

"I give the orders, sssslave!" Slappy hissed. "You will obey me. Obey me *forever!* Or you will pay!"

"Let go! Let me go!" I shrieked. I tugged. I struggled to my feet. I jerked my arms up and down.

But Slappy didn't loosen his hold.

His whole body bounced in the air. Hit the floor. Bounced back up as I pulled.

But his hands gripped even harder.

I couldn't free myself. And the pain — the intense pain — shot down my arms. Down my sides. Down my whole body.

"Pick me up, sssslave!" the dummy hissed. "Pick me up and put me on my chair."

"Let go!" I cried. "You're breaking my wrists! Let go!"

The dummy uttered a cold laugh in reply.

The pain shot through my body. My legs wobbled. I dropped back to my knees.

I turned in time to see Dan dive toward us.

I thought he was going to grab the dummy's hand and try to set me free.

Instead, Dan grabbed for the jacket pocket.

Slappy let go of my wrists. But not in time.

Dan pulled the slip of paper from the pocket.

Slappy swiped at Dan's hand, trying to grab the paper away.

But Dan swung around. He unfolded the paper and raised it to his face. And then he shouted out the mysterious words that were written there:

"Karru marri odonna loma molonu karrano."

Would it work?

Would it put Slappy back to sleep?

29

I rubbed my aching wrists and stared down at the grinning dummy.

He gazed back at me. And then winked.

His laughter roared over the thunder, over the hard, steady drumming of rain on the roof.

"You cannot defeat me that way, slave!" Slappy cried gleefully.

I took a step back. A chill ran down my back, making my whole body shudder.

My plan hadn't worked.

My only plan. My last, desperate plan. A total failure.

I caught the disappointment on Dan's face. The slip of paper fell from his fingers and floated to the floor.

"You will pay for this!" Slappy threatened. "You will pay for your foolish attempt to defeat me."

He pushed his hands against the floor and started to climb to his feet.

I backed up.

And saw the other dummies move.

All of them. They were sliding off their chairs. Lowering themselves from the couch.

They stretched their skinny arms. Flexed their big, wooden hands.

Their heads bobbed, their knees bent as they started to shuffle toward us.

They had all come to life! Twelve dummies, brought to life by those strange words Dan had cried out.

Twelve dummies staggering toward Dan and me.

We were trapped between them. Trapped in the circle as they shuffled, dragging their heavy shoes. Their eyes wide. Locked on Dan and me.

As they staggered and shuffled. Moving stiffly, grinning, grinning so coldly.

Closing in on Dan and me.

30

Wilbur limped toward us, his big, chipped hands stretched out, ready to grab us. Lucy's big blue eyes gleamed coldly as she staggered toward us. Arnie let out a high-pitched giggle as he pulled himself closer.

Closer.

Dan and I spun around. But we had nowhere to turn. Nowhere to escape.

The dummies' big shoes scraped heavily over the wooden floorboards. Their knees bent with each step. They looked as if they would tumble to the floor.

But they kept coming. Lurching forward. Bodies bending. Heads bobbing.

Alive. Wooden creatures. Alive!

Dan raised his hands over his face as if to shield himself.

I took a step back. But the dummies behind me were closing in, too.

I took a long, deep breath and held it.

Then I waited.

Waited for their wooden hands to grab us.

I uttered a loud gasp as Wilbur and Arnie staggered right past me.

The dummies all brushed past Dan and me.

As if we weren't there.

I stared in shock as they circled Slappy. I saw Rocky grab Slappy by the collar. I saw Lucy grab Slappy's shoes.

Then the circle of dummies moved in closer. Tighter.

I couldn't see what they were doing to Slappy. But I saw their skinny arms jerking and tugging. I saw them all struggling together.

Wrestling with him.

Were they pulling him apart?

I couldn't see. But I heard Slappy's scream of terror.

Dan and I clung to each other, watching the strange sight. It looked like a football huddle. A huddle of dummies.

The dummies grunted and groaned, muttering in low tones as they worked over Slappy.

We couldn't see Slappy in the middle.

We heard only one scream.

We didn't hear him scream again.

And then I heard the attic door open.

Footsteps on the stairs!

Someone was coming up.

31

I poked Dan and turned him to the stairs.

We both cried out as Zane climbed up to the attic and squinted across the long room at us.

Did he see the struggling dummies? Did he see that they were all alive?

I turned back — in time to see the dummies all collapse in a heap.

"Whoa!" I cried, my heart pounding. I blinked several times. I didn't believe what I saw.

The twelve dummies lay lifeless on the floor, arms and legs in a wild tangle. Mouths open. Eyes gazing up blankly at the low ceiling.

Slappy lay sprawled in the middle. His head tilted to one side. I saw the blank stare in his eyes. Saw the open-mouthed, wooden grin.

He was completely lifeless now. As lifeless as all the others.

Had the other dummies somehow destroyed his evil?

Would Slappy remain a lifeless block of wood forever?

I didn't have time to think about it. Zane came hurrying across the attic, an angry scowl on his face. His eyes were on the pile of dummies.

"Caught you!" Zane cried to Dan and me. "Caught you both! Planning your next trick! I *knew* you two were the ones! I'm telling Uncle Danny what you're doing!"

32

Of course no one believed Dan and me.

Of course everyone believed Zane.

We were in the worst trouble of our lives. Dan and I were grounded forever. We probably won't be allowed to leave the house until we are in our forties!

The next day, Zane and Uncle Cal were at the front door, saying good-bye. It's a terrible thing to say — but Dan and I were *not* sad to see Zane go.

"I hope I never have to come back here," he whispered to me in the hall. Then he put on a big, phony smile for Mom and Dad.

"Zane, what kind of camera would you like?" Dad asked, putting a hand on Zane's shoulder. "You have a birthday coming up. I'd like to send you a new camera for your birthday."

Zane shrugged his big shoulders. "Thanks," he told my Dad. "But I'm really not into photography anymore."

Mom and Dad raised their eyebrows in surprise.

"Well, what *would* you like for your birthday, Zane?" Mom asked. "Is there something else you're interested in?"

Zane shyly lowered his eyes to the floor. "Well . . . I'd kind of like to try being a ventriloquist — like you, Uncle Danny."

Dad beamed happily.

That creep Zane had said just the right thing.

"Maybe you have a spare dummy you can lend Zane," Uncle Cal suggested.

Dad rubbed his chin. "Well . . . maybe I do." He turned to me. "Trina, run up to the attic. And pick out a good dummy for Zane to take home. Not one of the old ones. But a nice one that Zane can enjoy."

"No problem, Dad," I replied eagerly. I hurried up to the attic. I hoped they didn't see the enormous grin on my face.

Can you guess which dummy I picked out for Zane?

I know it's horribly mean. But I really had no choice — did I?

"Here's a good one, Zane," I said a few seconds later. I placed the grinning dummy in Zane's arms. "His name is Slappy. I think you two will be very happy together."

I hope Zane has fun learning to be a ventrilo-quist.

But I have the feeling he may have a few prob-lems. Because as Zane carried Slappy into the car, I saw the dummy wink at me.

About the Author

R. L. Stine is the author of over three dozen best-selling thrillers and mysteries for young people. Recent titles for teenagers include *I Saw You That Night!*, *Call Waiting*, *Halloween Night II*, *The Dead Girlfriend*, and *The Baby-sitter IV*, all published by Scholastic. He is also the author of the *Fear Street* series.

Bob lives in New York City with his wife, Jane, and fifteen-year-old son, Matt.

Add *more*

Goosebumps®

to your collection . . .
A chilling preview of
what's next from
R.L. STINE

BAD HARE DAY

7

I grabbed Ginny by the arm and yanked her out the front door.

"What are you doing up?" I demanded.

"I was waiting for you to come into my room and turn me into a rabbit," she replied. "Or pretend to, anyway."

"I'm not going to do that tonight," I said. "Go back to bed."

"What are *you* doing up? Where are you going?"

I sat on the front steps and pulled on my sneakers. "Out to the garage," I lied. "To practice a new trick."

"You are not. I know where you're going. To Midnight Mansion!"

I grabbed her by the shoulders. "Okay. You're right. I'm going to Midnight Mansion. Don't tell Mom and Dad — promise?"

"I want to go!" she insisted. "Let me go with you."

"No. Go back to bed — and don't tell. Or you'll be sorry."

"You *have* to take me!" she declared. "If you don't, I'll run upstairs and tell Mom and Dad right now. Then you'll never get to see Amaz-O."

"You wouldn't."

"I would."

I knew she would.

"All right," I agreed. "You can come. But you have to be good and do everything I tell you to do."

"Maybe I will — and maybe I won't."

I sighed. I had to take her, no matter how bratty she was. If I did, she'd never tell — because then she'd be in as much trouble as me.

"Let's go," I whispered.

We sneaked into the garage and got our bikes. Then we pedaled off into the night.

It felt strange riding down Bank Street late at night. The shops were all closed and dark. Hardly any traffic on the street.

Oh, no. A police car up ahead — cruising toward us down Bank Street. If he spotted us, he'd stop us for sure. And then he'd take us home. And then we'd *really* be in trouble.

I searched desperately for a place to hide. The police couldn't miss us — Bank Street was lined with streetlights.

"Ginny!" I called. "Quick — out of the light!" I swerved into the dark doorway of a dress shop.

Ginny followed. We leaped off our bikes and pressed ourselves into the shadows.

The police car glided past. I held my breath as the headlights brushed across us. The car stopped.

"He saw us!" Ginny whispered. "Run!"

I grabbed her arm to stop her. "Wait." I peeked out into the street.

The police car was idling, but the driver stayed inside.

"It's a red light," I told Ginny. A few seconds later the light turned green, and the police car rolled away.

"We're safe now," I said. We hopped back onto our bikes and rode off.

Midnight Mansion loomed huge and dark at the edge of town. People said that a crazy old woman had lived alone in the mansion for forty years. She was rich, but so stingy she wore ragged old clothes and ate nothing but peanut butter, right out of the jar.

When people tried to visit her, she screamed, "Go away!" and threw rocks at them. She had about fifty cats. When she died, a businessman bought the mansion and turned it into a nightclub.

I braked in front of the old house and stared at it. Midnight Mansion.

It looked like a spooky old castle made of sooty black stone. Three stories tall, with two towers shooting up into the night sky. Vines crept across the roof. A floodlight threw creepy shadows over the house.

I'd seen the mansion a million times before. But late at night it looked bigger and darker than usual. I thought I saw bats fluttering around the two towers.

"No wonder the old lady went crazy," Ginny whispered. "Living in a spooky place like that."

"Do you think she kept prisoners in those towers?" I wondered.

"I think she had a torture chamber in the basement," Ginny said.

We walked our bikes up to the entrance. People hurried inside to see Amaz-O's magic show. Three men in long black capes breezed past us. A woman with long black hair, black lipstick, and pointy black fingernails smiled at me.

"Where did all these weird people come from?" Ginny asked.

I shrugged. "Let's go in. The show is about to start."

We locked our bikes and ran up the long stone steps. We entered a big hall lit by a crystal chandelier. We crossed the hall to a doorway covered by a heavy red curtain.

A tall, thin man in a black tuxedo guarded the curtain. He reached out a long, bony finger to stop us.

He had no hair, a pencil neck, and dark, hollow

eye sockets. "He looks like a skeleton," Ginny whispered to me.

I pulled the two tickets out of my back pocket and handed them to him.

"Very good," he croaked in a low voice. "But where are your parents? I can't seat children without their parents."

My parents? Think fast, Swanz-O, I told myself. "Um — my parents. Yes. Well, my parents, you see . . ." I had a feeling he didn't want to hear that my parents were home sleeping.

"They're outside, parking the car," I lied. "They'll be here in a minute. They told us to come in and get a table."

The man's hollow black eyes seemed to burn a hole in my brain. Would he buy it?

"I don't like it. But all right." He led us through the red curtain. The houselights went down just as we walked in. He showed us to a table right next to the stage.

"Excellent!" I said to Ginny as we sat down. "The best seats in the whole place!"

"This is so exciting!" she exclaimed. "I can't believe we're in a real, grown-up nightclub. By ourselves!"

The eerie-looking host stood by the red curtain, watching us. "We may not be here long," I warned her. "That skeleton guy's got his eye on us. When he realizes we're not here with our parents — "

"Shh! The show's starting."

A voice came over a loudspeaker. "Ladies and gentlemen! Midnight Mansion is proud to present the most famous magician in America. The fabulous, the incredible, the mind-boggling Amaz-O!"

A drum roll, and then horns bleating "Ta da!" The audience clapped and cheered. The curtain rose.

I gasped when I saw the stage. It was filled with wonderful equipment — a tall, shiny black box with a door in the front, a platform suspended from the ceiling, a glittering box with holes in it for a head, arms, and legs to stick out of. And a big white rabbit sitting beside a vase of blue flowers on a table covered with a red scarf.

The rabbit wasn't tied up or caged or anything. "I wonder how he keeps that rabbit from running away," Ginny whispered. "That's a trick *you* need to learn."

"You're so funny, Ginny," I said, rolling my eyes. "My sides are splitting with laughter."

"You have no sense of humor," Ginny jeered. "That's your problem."

"No. *You're* my problem," I snapped.

Amaz-O strode onstage. He was tall and slim, and his top hat made him seem even taller. He had long black hair and wore a black cape lined with red satin over a black tuxedo.

He tossed the cape over his shoulders and ᵔd.

I can't believe I'm seeing Amaz-O in person! I thought, my heart pounding with excitement. And so close — I could almost touch him!

Maybe I'll even see how some of his tricks are done, I thought. Maybe, sitting so close, I'll catch some of his secrets!

Without saying a word, Amaz-O scanned the audience. He trained his eyes on me.

My whole body shook. He's staring right at me! I gasped.

Amaz-O took a step forward and leaned toward me.

What's he doing? I thought. Is he going to talk to me?

Amaz-O leaned closer. His face was right next to mine! I cowered in my seat.

He scowled and whispered in a deep, menacing voice, "Disappear! Disappear!"

GET
Goosebumps®
by R.L. Stine

❑ BAB48346-3	**#34**	**Revenge of the Lawn Gnomes**	**$3.50**
❑ BAB48340-4	**#35**	**A Shocker on Shock Street**	**$3.50**
❑ BAB56873-6	**#36**	**The Haunted Mask II**	**$3.99**
❑ BAB56874-4	**#37**	**The Headless Ghost**	**$3.99**
❑ BAB56875-2	**#38**	**The Abominable Snowman of Pasadena**	**$3.99**
❑ BAB56876-0	**#39**	**How I Got My Shrunken Head**	**$3.99**
❑ BAB56877-9	**#40**	**Night of the Living Dummy III**	**$3.99**
❑ BAB56644-X		**Goosebumps 1996 Calendar**	**$9.95**
❑ BAB62836-4		**Book & Light Set: Tales to Give You The Creeps - Ten Spooky Stories**	**$11.95**
❑ BAB26603-9		**Book & Light Set #2: More Tales to Give You Goosebumps**	**$11.95**
❑ BAB55323-2		**Give Yourself Goosebumps Book #1: Escape from the Carnival of Horrors**	**$3.50**
❑ BAB56645-8		**Give Yourself Goosebumps Book #2: Tick Tock, You're Dead**	**$3.99**
❑ BAB56646-6		**Give Yourself Goosebumps Book #3: Trapped in Bat Wing Hall**	**$3.99**
❑ BAB53770-9		**The Goosebumps Monster Blood Pack**	**$11.95**
❑ BAB50995-0		**The Goosebumps Monster Sound Chip Book**	**$12.95**
❑ BAB60265-9		**Goosebumps Official Collector's Caps Collecting Kit**	**$5.99**

Scare me, thrill me, mail me GOOSEBUMPS now!

Available wherever you buy books, or use this order form. Scholastic Inc., P.O. Box 7502,
2931 East McCarty Street, Jefferson City, MO 65102

Please send me the books I have checked above. I am enclosing $_____ (please add
$2.00 to cover shipping and handling). Send check or money order — no cash or C.O.D.s please.

Name _____ Age _____

Address _____

City _____ State/Zip _____

Please allow four to six weeks for delivery. Offer good in the U.S. only. Sorry, mail orders are not available to
residents of Canada. Prices subject to change.